"I know your type."

"What's my type?"

"You're beautiful."

Tessa spun toward him, her mouth falling open at his compliment.

Desire caught in Chad's chest. He wanted to kiss her. "Vivacious," he continued. "Reckless."

"I am not reckless."

"Your driving record proves otherwise."

She shrugged. "A few speeding tickets. And I'm not reckless. You *don't* know me."

"You're wrong," he murmured as she ground the engine, then peeled out of the ramp with such speed the gate rattled. "I know you, Tessa Howard."

Dear Reader,

I am so excited to be starting a new series for Harlequin American Romance—CITIZEN'S POLICE ACADEMY, based on my participation in the Grand Rapids, Michigan, Citizen Police Academy. The police department sponsors this program to educate the community about how they operate. I learned a lot, but most of all I developed such appreciation and understanding for how difficult and dangerous a career in law enforcement is. The people who choose these careers are very special.

While the officers in the Lakewood Police Department are purely fictional, I've imbued them with some of the sterling qualities of the officers I met in the GRPD. And I can't wait to give each of these characters the happily-ever-after they deserve.

Once a Lawman is also part of the MEN MADE IN AMERICA miniseries, a yearlong celebration of American heroes. In 2009 look for one book a month that celebrates the hunky American male!

Happy reading!

Lisa Childs

Once a Lawman
LISA CHILDS

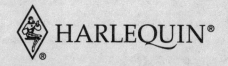

HARLEQUIN®

TORONTO • NEW YORK • LONDON
AMSTERDAM • PARIS • SYDNEY • HAMBURG
STOCKHOLM • ATHENS • TOKYO • MILAN • MADRID
PRAGUE • WARSAW • BUDAPEST • AUCKLAND

Recycling programs
for this product may
not exist in your area.

ISBN-13: 978-0-373-75249-2
ISBN-10:   0-373-75249-0

ONCE A LAWMAN

Copyright © 2009 by Lisa Childs-Theeuwes.

www.eHarlequin.com

Printed in U.S.A.

ABOUT THE AUTHOR

Bestselling, award-winning author Lisa Childs writes paranormal and contemporary romance for Harlequin/Silhouette Books. She lives on thirty acres in west Michigan with her husband, two daughters, a talkative Siamese and a long-haired Chihuahua who thinks she's a rottweiler. Lisa loves hearing from readers who can contact her through her Web site, www.lisachilds.com, or by snail-mail at P.O. Box 139, Marne, MI 49435.

Books by Lisa Childs

HARLEQUIN AMERICAN ROMANCE

1198—UNEXPECTED BRIDE
1210—THE BEST MAN'S BRIDE
1222—FOREVER HIS BRIDE
1230—FINALLY A BRIDE

HARLEQUIN NEXT

TAKING BACK MARY ELLEN BLACK
LEARNING TO HULA
CHRISTMAS PRESENCE
  "Secret Santa"

HARLEQUIN INTRIGUE

664—RETURN OF THE LAWMAN
720—SARAH'S SECRETS
758—BRIDAL RECONNAISSANCE
834—THE SUBSTITUTE SISTER

A special thank-you to Watch Commander, Lieutenant Mark Ostapowicz, of the Grand Rapids Police Department, for his patience and helpfulness in answering my many, many questions while I was a participant in the Citizen Police Academy and my many questions in the course of writing this book. Any factual mistakes are entirely my fault.

And much gratitude to Kathleen Scheibling for contracting this series of my heart for Harlequin American Romance.

Chapter One

Tessa Howard glanced around the courtroom, crowded with whispering people of all walks of life: elderly, teenagers and young professionals like herself. The knot of tension in her stomach eased. *He* wasn't going to show up. *I'm almost free.*

Maybe taking the time to fight her ticket in traffic court hadn't been wasted. If the officer who'd given her the ticket failed to show up, the speeding charge would be dropped. She glanced at her watch, the knot of tension tightening again as she thought of the appointments she was missing. While she couldn't afford the time waiting in court was taking, she could afford another ticket even less.

"Tessa Howard," the bailiff called her to the bench.

Tessa stood, refastened the button on her suit jacket, and tugged down the skirt that had ridden up her thighs. She swung her straight blond hair over her shoulder. The hair flip, as usual, attracted male attention. From her career in telecommunication sales—and her maternal grandmother—Tessa had learned that a smart woman used her brains and her femininity to get what she wanted. Of course, neither of them had gotten her out of her ticket. Yet.

She drew in a deep breath. After crawling over the other people in her row, she stepped into the aisle and, heels clicking on the tile floor, approached the bench.

"You're in my court again, Ms. Howard," the judge commented as she approached. "Speeding?"

"No, sir, I wasn't speeding. The officer must have confused my car with someone else's," she insisted. What was it that Nana Howard had always claimed? *A lie well told and stuck to is just as good as the truth.*

Her grandmother had freely imparted her sometimes unconventional bits of wisdoms. Nana-isms had probably prepared Tessa more for her career than the marketing classes at Lakewood Community College had.

A smile tugged up the corner of the judge's mouth, softening the older man's austere face. "Is that true, Lieutenant Michalski?"

Tessa's heart skipped a beat. She'd thought she was home free, that the uptight lieutenant had been too busy to make her little court date...

Her pulse quickened as she realized he stood right beside her, his long, muscular body clad in the black uniform of the Lakewood, Michigan Police Department. She tilted her head to see his face.

He'd lost the sunglasses he'd worn the day he had pulled her over, but still she couldn't see his eyes. He stared straight ahead, as completely uninterested in her as he had been when he'd given her the ticket. She hadn't been able to flirt her way out of this violation, as she had some others.

"Lieutenant Michalski?" the judge prodded him.

"Ms. Howard's SUV was the only vehicle within radar range. She was definitely the one speeding."

"I wasn't going as fast as you said," she persisted.

"Eleven miles over the speed limit," he stated unequivocally—and correctly.

"But eleven miles…" Wasn't that many over the limit—it certainly wasn't as reckless as he had claimed it was. She would *never* drive recklessly. Too many people depended on her.

"Eleven miles over is still speeding, Ms. Howard. The ticket stands," the judge ruled. "Pay your fine."

"Your Honor, please," she beseeched him. "I had a good reason for speeding." Which she had tried to tell Lieutenant Michalski, but he hadn't cared.

"So now you *were* speeding, Ms. Howard? A minute ago you assured me you weren't," the judge reminded her.

"But…" She bit her lip and refrained from explaining that her mother's car had broken down. As the lieutenant had said when she'd offered him the excuse, her mother should have called the Auto Club instead of Tessa.

But Tessa actually had been on the way to pick up her younger brother, Kevin, not her mother. Recognizing an unsympathetic listener, she hadn't bothered explaining about her teenage brother and that if someone didn't pick him up from high school, he would disappear for the night, getting into only God knew what trouble.

She doubted the court would be any more sympathetic than the police officer. And she doubted it was a good idea to mention her brother to the authorities at all, especially now. So far he had avoided getting into trouble with the law, and dealt just with school and *her* for tardiness and skipping classes.

"Yes, Ms. Howard?" the judge prodded her.

She released her lip and admitted, "If I get any more tickets on my record, the Secretary of State will pull my license."

"Considering her driving record, losing her license would

probably be a good thing," the lieutenant commented, staring straight ahead.

"But if I lose my license, I'll lose my job," she said, as panic shortened her breath. "I can't afford to lose my job…" For so many reasons. Hers wasn't the only head over which she had to keep a roof.

"You should have considered that before you started speeding, Ms. Howard," the judge remarked with no sympathy.

"May I make a suggestion, Your Honor?" the police officer asked.

The judge's eyes narrowed warily, but then he nodded. "Of course you may, Lieutenant Michalski."

"Maybe the citation, and the subsequent loss of her license, isn't the most fitting punishment for Ms. Howard's violation."

"You gave me the ticket," she whispered, sending him a glare, which she doubted he would see. But he had finally turned toward her, his gaze intent on her face. His eyes were green, with flecks of gold. With his black hair, she had figured they'd be brown or blue. She shook her head, disgusted that she had spent so much time—time she didn't have to spare— thinking about *his* eyes.

"You have a more suitable punishment?" the judge asked him.

"More education than punishment," the lieutenant alluded, "I think Ms. Howard could learn a lot about obeying speed limits and the law in general if she were to enroll in Lakewood Police Department's Citizens' Police Academy."

The judge leaned back, a grin spreading across his face. "Interesting…"

"What—how?" she stammered, lifting her palms up. "I don't even know what the Citizens' Police Academy is. I don't want to be a police officer."

"It's not the *police* academy," the lieutenant assured her, grinning slightly as if he were amused. "It won't make you a police officer, although some people enroll to see if they might want to pursue a career in law enforcement. It will help you understand police procedure—the how and why."

Like why certain police officers were too rigid to let a driver off with just a warning? She bit her lip again so she wouldn't ask the question. No sense antagonizing him when he seemed to be changing his mind about the ticket.

"It's a great program," the judge enthused. "The Lakewood PD Watch Commander, Lieutenant O'Donnell, has been putting it on for a few years to promote community involvement and relations. The chief and the city council have made certain there's money in the budget for it, so there's no charge for the public to participate. Some officers have been known to donate their time just to make certain it doesn't go over budget."

Did Lieutenant Michalski donate his time? Would he be part of the program?

"It sounds interesting," she belatedly agreed with the judge to humor him. In truth, she didn't have any interest in the program or Lieutenant Michalski.

"Then you'll agree to enroll?"

"I would, but I have a job," she reminded them. At least she did for now. "I can't afford to miss any time from work."

"The CPA meets only one night a week," the lieutenant explained. "Wednesdays from six-thirty to ten for fifteen weeks."

Tessa's breath caught. Fifteen weeks. "I really—"

"Don't have a choice if you want to keep your license," the judge pointed out. "The ticket or the class, Ms. Howard?"

"The class," she begrudgingly replied. Then she reminded herself what one more ticket would have cost her. "Thank you, Your Honor."

"Don't thank me," the judge said, "It was the lieutenant's idea."

She turned toward her benefactor. "Thank you."

While his jaw remained taut, his mouth unsmiling, his green eyes brightened—no doubt with more amusement at her expense, over the predicament she was in. "You'll enjoy the class, Ms. Howard."

"I doubt that."

"I won't be participating," he assured her.

She smiled. "Then maybe I will…"

"YOU'RE GOING to have to participate," the watch commander, Lieutenant Patrick O'Donnell, told Chad, his back to him as he climbed the steps to his office, the glass walls of which rose above the reception area where interns sat at the front desk, taking nonemergency calls and buzzing in visitors.

Chad followed him, protesting, "Paddy—"

"You're the emergency vehicle operation instructor for the police department," the commander pointed out, as he settled into the chair behind his counter-height, U-shaped desk, "as well as for the Lakewood University's Police Academy."

"Yeah, the *police* academy—"

"Now you're the instructor for the *citizens'* police academy, too," Paddy said. His eyes, nearly the same reddish brown as his hair, crinkled at the corners as he grinned.

While they were both lieutenants, being watch commander gave Paddy more authority. He doled out assignments. Chad couldn't turn one down—even though police participation in the program was *supposed* to be voluntary.

"Hey, you've been recruiting for the class," Paddy reminded him, "You should help."

Although Chad leaned against the doorjamb, he couldn't

relax—he hadn't been able to since he'd first pulled over a black SUV driven by a certain blue-eyed blonde. "I only recruited one person."

"Tessa Howard." The watch commander never forgot a name. "What's the story with her?"

Chad shrugged tense shoulders. "Nothing. I gave her a ticket for speeding. She tried to fight it in traffic court."

"And lost?"

"She would have lost her license…" And she probably should have. Before giving her the ticket, he'd run her record and had seen all her speeding warnings and citations—one for going too fast for conditions that had resulted in a minor property damage accident.

"So you talked the judge into enrolling her in the class instead of giving her a ticket?" Paddy whistled with surprise. "I've never known you to let anyone off a ticket."

Chad mentally kicked himself for stepping in with his *brilliant* suggestion. Now if anything happened to Ms. Howard, it was his fault. His idea made her *his* responsibility now. He straightened. "I just thought she'd learn a lot from the class and that she might come to understand how reckless speeding is." He was actually counting on it.

"If you teach the traffic/defensive driving session of the class, she will," Paddy said. "You can *personally* explain to her the consequences of speeding."

Because he'd lived with—or actually *without*—the consequences? Chad shook his head. "No. I would never get *personal* with Tessa Howard."

"Junior—" Chad wasn't actually a junior, but because of his reputation as an expert driver, he'd been nicknamed Dale Earnhardt, Jr. "The problem is that you don't get personal with anyone," the commander continued, "not since your wife died."

Chad sucked in a breath. Although it had been four years since Luanne's death, those last three words struck him like a battering ram in the gut. He still missed her—what they'd had and what they could have had—what they *should* have had.

"It's been a long time, Chad," Paddy said, his deep voice soft with sympathy and understanding.

Chad nodded. "Yeah. Sometimes too long. Sometimes not long enough…" For the loss to stop hurting.

Paddy's eyes locked on Chad's. "It's been long enough. Luanne would have wanted you to move on."

She probably would have, but Chad wasn't ready. He doubted he'd ever be ready.

"How long you been divorced, Paddy?" he asked his friend.

The watch commander dropped his gaze to his desk as he shuffled some files. "That's different."

"Yeah." Paddy could see his ex again whereas Luanne was gone forever. If only she hadn't been speeding that day… He'd warned her so many times to slow down.

He was kidding himself to think Tessa Howard would learn anything in the academy. If he hadn't been able to get through to his own wife, how would he get through to her? "This was a bad idea."

"What was?" Paddy asked distractedly as he shoveled through the files on his desk. The radio next to a flat-screen monitor crackled with the dispatcher's voice sending out units on the latest 911 calls. Messages also flashed across the screen. The watch commander divided his attention between the calls and the files. But from the half-empty coffee mugs on his desk and atop the file cabinets, he was used to people dropping by his office to talk, too.

So Chad didn't feel too badly for taking up his time. "I

should have kept my mouth shut in court." He sighed. "Hell, I probably shouldn't have shown up at all."

"The judge would have thrown out the ticket then."

"He threw it out anyway." Because of Chad's interference. He pushed a hand through his hair. "Do you really need my help with the academy?"

Paddy looked up from his paperwork, his eyes narrowed. Then he nodded. "I can't wait to meet Ms. Howard."

"It's not like that…"

"Like what?" Paddy asked. "She isn't young and pretty?"

"She's twenty-seven," he recalled from her license, which had actually had a good picture—although he couldn't imagine her taking a bad one. "So yeah, she's young." He glanced at his watch, but he didn't have anyplace to go. His shift had ended.

"And pretty?"

She wasn't *just* pretty. With her spunk and sass, she was so much more. Thinking of her bright blue eyes and golden blond hair, *gorgeous* was the word that most readily sprang to his mind. Since the day he had pulled her over, he had thought about her—too much. The way she had batted her thick black lashes and had spoken in a breathy voice, trying to flirt her way out of the ticket. Then in court, the way she'd gnawed her bottom lip…

He suppressed a groan and lied to the watch commander, "I hadn't noticed."

Paddy laughed, knowing him so well that he had to realize Chad lied. "Well, helping me out as one of the class instructors will give you time to notice."

"She probably won't even show up." He hoped.

His STOMACH FLIPPED as Tessa Howard, blond hair swinging around her shoulders, settled onto a chair at the table in the front row—just feet away from where Chad Michalski sat with the other instructors. While most of the rest of the class had dressed casually in either jeans or khakis and sweaters or sweatshirts, Tessa wore a suit similar to the one she'd worn in court. A tailored, pinstriped navy blue jacket cinched her slim waist while a slim pencil skirt ended above her knees but inched farther up her thighs as she crossed her legs.

Chad swallowed hard and shifted on his chair. If only he'd kept quiet in court…

The watch commander nudged his shoulder. "Tessa Howard?"

He nodded.

"Now I understand why—"

Chad nudged him back. "Don't you have a class to teach?"

Paddy grinned, but stood up and addressed the group of citizens and instructors gathered in the third-floor meeting room. "Welcome to the Lakewood Police Department's Citizens' Police Academy."

Welcome? Tessa bit her bottom lip to hold in a chuckle. *Welcome* implied she attended the class of her own free will. Her attention shifted from the man standing before the table at the front of the spacious, white-walled, low-ceilinged room to one of the men sitting behind the table. Her gaze locked with Lieutenant Chad Michalski's.

"Oh, good choice," murmured the girl beside Tessa. She leaned closer as if they were passing notes in class. "He's single, too. I already checked. He's a little old for me, though, but he sure is yummy."

Tessa snorted although she wasn't certain to what she'd taken exception—the lieutenant being called yummy or old. He definitely wasn't old; she estimated early thirties, at the most. He continued to stare at her, his jaw taut probably with disapproval, as if she were the one talking during class. Be-

cause she'd been late, she'd had no choice of where to sit—
the chair next to the young girl at the first table had been the
only one still vacant.

"We're going to go around the room and have everyone introduce themselves," the officer continued. He was obviously
the leader of the class. From the e-mail she had received with
the date, time and directions to the police department, she had
learned his name was Lieutenant Patrick O'Donnell. "And
then I'll introduce the other instructors. A little later we'll
meet the chief of police and the district captains."

Tessa had lived her entire twenty-seven years in Lakewood,
Michigan, but yet she had no idea how many districts com-
prised the bustling, midsized city. The only contact she'd had
with the police department, besides getting and paying for
tickets, had been when she'd tried to sign them up for their
phone and Internet service accounts.

O'Donnell stepped forward and rapped his knuckles
against the table at which Tessa sat, her briefcase propped
against her chair. "Let's start with this table."

With a giggle, the young girl spoke up. "My name's Amy,
Amy Wilson. I'm a college student, and I joined the academy
because I'm interested in law enforcement."

Tessa held in another derisive snort. The girl was obviously
more interested in law enforcers than enforcement. The dark-
haired woman on the other side of Tessa smiled, apparently
having drawn the same conclusion. Lieutenant O'Donnell
nodded at Tessa to introduce herself. "Tessa Howard. I'm a
sales rep for a telecommunications company."

"And your reason for joining the academy?" he prodded.

She glanced at Chad, who smirked. The truth stuck in her
throat, so she smiled and joked, "I thought maybe I'd get
some inside information on where the speed traps are."

The class and some of the instructors chuckled. But not Chad. The slight grin dropped from his handsome face, and his green eyes hardened with definite disapproval. The guy had no sense of humor.

It was going to be a *long* fifteen weeks…

"I'M SURPRISED you showed up," a deep voice murmured close to her ear as Tessa waited for the elevator. She tensed, realizing she was alone with him. The third floor of the police department was deserted except for the two of them. She'd had to take a call, so she'd missed walking out with the rest of the class. Heck, she had missed whatever had happened after the last break since she had stayed in the restroom, on the phone.

"I wasn't given much choice," she reminded him as she jabbed the Down button again. If she knew where the stairs were, she would have already been in the lobby. Her phone vibrated, then chimed as she received a text.

"You could have chosen to accept the ticket."

"And lose my license?" She shook her head as she pulled out her phone and read the message. "And my job? I had *no* choice."

"You do now."

"What do you mean?" she asked, turning toward him. She didn't dare hope that he had changed his mind, but she had to ask, "Are you going to let me out of the academy?"

Irritation furrowed his brow, and he pushed a hand through his dark hair. "No. The judge only agreed to this with the stipulation that you don't miss a single class."

"I won't—"

"You missed half the class." He reached for her and wrapped his fingers around her hand that held the cell. "Because of this."

Her skin tingling, Tessa pulled away just as the elevator doors finally slid open. She stepped inside and reached for the L button. So did he, his hand brushing hers again.

"I can't miss any calls," she said, but refrained from offering any further explanation. As the doors closed them into the small car together, Tessa drew in a shaky breath.

"It's one night. Just a few hours. You can return your missed calls later," he said, "not during class. The choice you have is to show up every week and either sit and pout, or participate."

She lifted her chin. "I don't pout."

"Sulk, then."

She opened then closed her mouth, unable to disagree with his observation. Thinking of what she was missing while at the academy, she had sulked.

"If you participate, you might find you learn something," he pointed out as the elevator stopped and the doors opened to the deserted lobby, "and enjoy yourself."

She might, but she wouldn't admit that to him. "The other people in class sound interesting," she said, thinking of the witty introductions of everyone from a reporter for the *Lakewood Chronicle*, the dark-haired woman sitting on the other side of her, some Neighborhood Watch captains, a couple of teachers, a youth minister, a former gang member turned youth center founder to an elderly couple who had admitted taking the class for thrills. Heck, even the mayor's daughter was taking the class although, given her reputation, her participation might not have been voluntary, either.

"And they're interested," the lieutenant persisted, "in learning."

"You don't think I am?" she asked.

He laughed, the corners of his eyes crinkling and etching

deep creases in his cheeks. Tessa's breath caught at the trans-formation. Maybe Amy was right; he was *yummy*.

"I know you're not interested."

Once again, she couldn't lie, so she just smiled. "Well, only fourteen more classes to go. See you next week, Lieutenant." She turned toward the doors to the street.

But he walked across the lobby with her, shortening his long strides to match hers. Then he pushed open the glass door.

"Thanks for seeing me out," she said as she passed through the doorway.

"Did you park in the ramp around the block?" he asked.

She nodded.

"I'll walk you to your car."

"That's not necessary."

"It's almost eleven," he pointed out as he followed her onto the sidewalk. Tall buildings, the windows dark after hours, flanked the cobblestone street. "This isn't the safest neighborhood at night."

"That's pretty ironic," she mused. "I would have figured the neighborhood around the police department would be the safest place in the city."

"You'd figure, huh?" he agreed as he stepped closer as if shielding her with his body.

Even though he didn't touch her, Tessa's skin tingled again. She shook her head, disgusted with herself for acting as hor-monal as the barely-out-of-her-teens, police-groupie Amy. Even if Tessa did go for men in uniform, this would be the last man to whom she would be attracted.

"Is it because of the jail?" she asked. "Why it isn't safe here?"

"Booking and lock-up is in a separate building, blocks away," he assured her. "But there are some muggers and car thieves who prey on the after-theater and bar crowd."

"Well, I'm not coming from the theater or a bar, so you really don't need to walk me to my car," she insisted, her heels clicking against the concrete as she quickened her pace. Despite it being early September, a brisk wind blew off Lake Michigan, which was only miles from downtown Lakewood, cooling the night air.

"Since the rest of the class left before you, I can't let you walk out alone here," he said, his voice thickening with some of the frustration she felt.

Shadows shifted around the buildings, and Tessa's grip tightened on her briefcase. "You take this whole serve-and-protect thing seriously."

"Protect and serve," Chad corrected her. "And yes, I do." That was the only reason he had suggested she enroll in the CPA—for her protection and the protection of everyone else on the road. Not because he was attracted to her. He could *not* be attracted to her. Yet his gaze skimmed down her body, over the wiggle of her hips as she stalked toward the parking garage in the high heels that brought the top of her blond head nearly to the level of his chin.

"Whatever," she said, dismissive of a police officer's sacred oath, "You take it too seriously."

He bit back a laugh as he followed her up the ramp of the parking garage. "I don't think I've ever met a more self-involved woman."

Her blond hair swayed across her back as she swung her head toward him. She gasped, and her blue eyes widened with surprise. "You think *I'm* self-involved?"

Thinking of her shameless flirting and constant phone calls and texts, he snorted. "I don't think. I *know* it."

"You don't *know* me at all," she said, heels slamming into the concrete as she stalked up the ramp.

"I know your type."

"What's my type?" she asked, but didn't even slow down for his answer.

He caught her arm, drawing her to a halt just steps from her black SUV, which she probably would have stormed right past. "You're beautiful."

She spun toward him, her mouth falling open at his compliment.

Desire kicked him in the ribs. He wanted to kiss her. "Vivacious," he continued. "Reckless." And that was why he couldn't kiss her. "With total disregard for your safety or anyone else's."

She pulled keys from her briefcase, her hand shaking so much that they jangled, and unlocked her SUV. "I am not reckless."

"Your driving record proves otherwise."

She shrugged. "A few speeding tickets."

"One with an accident," he reminded her.

She laughed, albeit without humor. "I hit a patch of black ice and slid off the road into a mailbox."

He tensed, dread tightening his stomach muscles. "It could have just as easily been a tree or utility pole."

"It wasn't." She lifted her chin. "And I didn't even put a dent in my vehicle."

"The mailbox wasn't so lucky," he pressed. "You need to slow down. Stop being so reckless…"

"I wasn't going fast. And I'm not reckless. You *don't* know me," she insisted as she pulled open the driver's door.

He nodded as if he agreed with her, even though he didn't. "Let's keep it that way."

As she planted her toe on the running board, Chad palmed her head, so she wouldn't hit the metal doorjamb. Her silky hair brushed his palm. She ducked her chin, pulling away from him, and her eyes darkened with anger. "*Let's* keep it that way," she agreed.

Chad winced as she started the SUV, grinding the engine, then peeled out of the ramp with such speed that the gate, raised after hours, rattled.

"You're wrong," he murmured. "I know you, Tessa Howard. I know I don't want anything to do with you…"

But to protect and serve. That was the oath by which he lived. His *only* reason for living now…

Chapter Two

Shaking from her argument with the lieutenant, Tessa fumbled with her keys to her ranch house. Before she could unlock the door, the knob turned beneath her palm and the door opened. She jumped back, startled.

"Gee, Tess—"

"What are you still doing up?" she asked her younger brother. Since summer vacation had just ended, getting him back in the habit of going to bed early hadn't been easy.

Christopher, clad in his superhero pajamas, stepped back from the doorway. "I just texted you a little while ago."

"When you should have been in bed," she admonished the ten-year-old as she joined him in the country kitchen with its warm oak cupboards and green-apple painted walls. "And what did I tell you about opening up that door without knowing who's on the other side?"

"I knew it was you," he said as he climbed onto a chair at the long oak trestle table. "I saw you drive up."

"You shouldn't have been waiting up for me."

"What was the police academy like?" he asked, his blue eyes bright with excitement as he stared up at her. "Did they let you shoot a gun?"

She bit her lip to hold back a smile. "No. It's not like that." At least she hoped not, because she should definitely *not* be trusted with a gun around the lieutenant. "It's the *citizens'* police academy."

"So what was it like?" Christopher asked, still awed. "What did you do in class?"

She shrugged. "Not much. It was just a bunch of people talking."

The chief had given a rather eloquent speech with a short question-and-answer period, and each district captain had talked about the areas for which they were responsible. Then the instructor for each session had been about to speak when she had slipped away to return her missed calls. From what she could tell so far, the purpose of the academy was to teach people how the police department and police officers worked, which would be fine if she had any interest, either. But she didn't. *No* interest in *any* police officer.

"Tess!" Christopher yelled as if he'd been trying to get her attention. "Did you ask if I can come next week?"

She shook her head. "No—"

"Tess!" The little boy's voice squeaked with indignation. "Why didn't you ask?"

"Because you *can't* come. The class isn't over until past your bedtime." Although Christopher was not much smaller than her, she lifted him from the chair. Her arms and back strained in protest of the exertion. She breathed deeply, inhaling the fruity scent of his shampoo. At least he'd had a bath, but it looked as if no one had untangled his mop of dish-water-blond curls. "And that's where you're going right now—to bed."

He wriggled out of her arms and protested, "I'm not a baby, Tess."

"You need your sleep. You should already be in bed," she reproached him, playfully swatting at his pajama-covered bottom as he headed down the hall.

"Audrey?" she called out in a loud whisper for her fourteen-year-old sister, who was supposed to have been watching the younger kids while their mother was at work and Tessa had been at the damn class she didn't have time to take. As Tessa had feared, Audrey wasn't responsible enough yet to handle the others. Besides Christopher and Audrey, there were three more kids.

Tessa poked her head into the first doorway off the hall, where Christopher climbed the ladder of a bunk bed to the top bed. On the bottom bunk slept their brother Joey, the blankets kicked off his small body. Tessa crept forward and pulled the covers to his chin, then pushed back his tangle of brown bangs and pressed a kiss against the five-year-old's forehead.

He murmured in his sleep. "Mommy…"

"No, she'll be home in the morning," she assured him as he drifted back to sleep. After tucking in Christopher, despite his protests, she headed back into the hall and collided with Audrey.

The dark-haired girl was already taller than Tessa, and should have been able to handle the younger kids at least. "Hey, Tess…"

"Where have you been?" she asked, then answered her own question. "On the computer, of course."

"I had to finish my homework." The girl's blue eyes narrowed in an accusatory glare. "*You* wouldn't help me."

Tessa had tried; she'd been on the phone with Audrey most of the second half of the class, when she hadn't been calling Kevin.

"Where's your older brother?" she asked. "Did he go out?" Even though Tessa had told him before she'd left for the police department that he couldn't?

Audrey shrugged. "I dunno."

Tessa sighed. If Mom let him get his license, like the sixteen-year-old wanted, they wouldn't be able to control the kid at all anymore. He came and went as he wanted *now,* with no regard to curfew. A headache began to throb at her temples. She would deal with Kevin later. "And Suzie?"

"She just got to sleep."

Probably because Audrey had kept the seven-year-old awake when she'd been using the computer in their shared bedroom. "You better go to bed, too," Tessa said.

"But my homework…" Audrey whined, her lips forming the pout of which the lieutenant had accused Tessa.

"You just said you finished it," she reminded the teenager.

"But you need to check it," Audrey insisted. "I'm barely passing algebra."

Like Tessa had a feeling she would barely pass her class if Lieutenant Michalski had his way. She had to talk him into releasing her from her court-ordered participation in the academy. As she walked back into the kitchen to the homework Audrey had left spread across the table, lights shone through the windows as a car pulled into the driveway. Her mother wouldn't be home for a few hours yet, not until after the bar closed. It had to be Kevin's ride dropping him off.

Neither Audrey nor Kevin was responsible enough to take care of the younger kids or themselves; the responsibility was all hers. Tessa had to figure a way out of the citizens' police academy.

"I'M GOING TO SKIP this week's class," Chad warned Paddy as he buttoned up his uniform shirt over the bulletproof vest Lakewood PD officers were required to wear every time they put on their uniform.

Other officers talked and slammed lockers shut as they, too, got ready for their shifts. The long, narrow basement room, with the gun-metal gray lockers and brick walls, reverberated with noise, but Chad suspected the watch commander had heard him and was just ignoring his pronouncement.

While Paddy sat on a bench tying his shoes, Chad glanced over at his friend's open locker. He noticed the other man had put up new school pictures of his kids, and Chad's heart contracted with a swift, sharp jab of pain.

He looked inside his own locker, at the pieces of tape stuck inside the door. The pictures were gone. After Luanne's death he'd taken down her photo. And after his premature son had died two weeks later, he'd taken down his sonogram picture. But he'd left the pieces of tape, as if he might someday have new pictures to post.

But Luanne was gone; their child was gone. Only the pain remained. He couldn't risk more pain; there would be *no* more pictures. He reached for one of the pieces of tape, picking at it with his fingernail.

Paddy stood and as he attached his gun, two extra magazine clips, Taser, collapsible baton, pepper spray and radio to his belt, he stared at the pictures of his kids. Since his divorce, he didn't see his children nearly as often as he liked.

But at least he could see them.

"I'm skipping the CPA class this week," Chad repeated, with enough volume that Paddy couldn't continue pretending to have not heard him.

"We've already been through this, Junior," the watch commander reminded him as he closed and leaned against his locker. "You're the resident emergency vehicle operation and traffic stop expert."

"You don't need an expert for this week's class," Chad protested, abandoning the stubborn tape. He would have to take care of it later. "You're just doing the tour of the department."

Paddy shook his head. "That won't take four hours. We're going to show some video footage, too. Give 'em a day in the life of a police officer."

"I thought that was the purpose of the ride-along."

"This week we do sign-ups for the ride-alongs," Paddy informed him. "The tapes give 'em an idea of what to expect."

Chad snorted. "*We* never know what to expect when we go out." A routine traffic stop could easily become a drug arrest, or a shoot-out. Or a confrontation with an unsettlingly beautiful woman.

"Ain't that the truth," Paddy agreed with a heavy sigh. "And that's why I like to share with them that you have to expect the unexpected. Hopefully it'll inspire them to be careful on their ride-alongs."

Chad inwardly groaned. Based on her speeding and her wanting to walk the city streets alone at night, Tessa Howard didn't have a clue about how to be careful. "Maybe you should skip the ride-alongs this session."

Paddy grinned. "Thinking about Tessa Howard?"

Too much, but he wasn't about to share that with the watch commander. "She's not the only one who might be a problem."

"The mayor's daughter," Paddy added with a derisive snort. "Who's probably spying for her daddy so he can find out where to cut our budget."

And politics like that was why Chad was happy in his present position. He wouldn't want Paddy's job or the public information officer's, either. "Erin Powell is in the class, too," he reminded the watch commander.

Paddy uttered a groan. "Kent's reporter is already a problem."

Erin Powell at the *Lakewood Chronicle* was determined to paint the department, but most especially Sergeant Kent Terlecki, the department's public information officer aka media liaison, in the worst light.

"Why did you approve her application for the academy?" Chad wondered. He would have asked about the reporter's admittance earlier, but he had been preoccupied with another member of the CPA.

Paddy shrugged. "I left it up to Kent."

So Chad wasn't the only one who had erred in judgment.

"Anyway, I need you to pull some traffic stop footage for me," Paddy continued.

"I can pull the footage," Chad agreed, "but I don't have to be there to show it."

"Yeah, you do," the watch commander insisted, "in case anyone has questions."

"With the reporter in the class, Kent should be the one answering all the questions."

"Maybe that's the reason he shouldn't," Paddy reasoned. "Did you read today's paper?"

"Not yet."

"Don't waste your time," Paddy advised him. "Hopefully Kent hasn't seen it, either."

"I'm sure he has." Chad doubted the public information officer missed any of Powell's articles.

"Then that's another reason you're not going to want to miss this week's class," Paddy predicted.

"Okay, I'll be there." If only for moral support for his fellow officer. Chad glanced at his watch and noted that he had some time before the night-shift briefing.

A few minutes later, he stepped out of the stairwell onto the second floor where the offices were located. He intended to talk to Kent, but another voice drew his attention—a fast-talking, feminine one.

"And you don't have to worry about one-eight-hundred numbers and automated answering services. You'll have my cell number and can reach me directly, any time day or night, if you have any problems," Tessa Howard assured the chief as the older man walked her out of his office. "Not that you'll have any problems. I'm sure you'll find our Internet and phone service much more reliable than your current carrier."

"I'll have to look over your proposal, Ms. Howard," Chief Archer stalled as he tapped a finger against the folder in his hand. "Then let you know my decision."

"I'll be here later this week for the citizens' police academy," she said. "I can come in early and check with you before the class starts."

"That's right. You're a member of the academy," Chief Archer said with a smile of obvious pride in the department.

"Not by choice," Chad chimed in, unwilling to let her use the CPA as a selling point. Wearing a short skirt and tight jacket again, she could have been in another type of profession. The lady was not above using any of her assets to get what she wanted, as he recalled from her shameless flirting during the traffic stop. "Well, actually I guess the judge *did* give her a choice—the academy or another speeding ticket."

"Hello, Lieutenant," the chief greeted him while Tessa just glared.

Chad ignored her and turned toward his boss, who was also a good friend. A year ago Frank Archer had joined Chad's unofficial club of widowers. Misery didn't quite love company but at least appreciated it. "Chief."

Archer studied him and Tessa, his brow furrowed in deep thought. "It appears you already know Ms. Howard."

Chad nodded. "Yes, I know Ms. Howard."

"Humph," Tessa said and murmured, "He only thinks he does."

"Then perhaps you two should get to know each other better," the chief suggested.

"No!" the protest slipped through Chad's lips.

"That's not necessary," Tessa said, leaving Chad to wonder if she referred to his reaction or to his getting to know her better.

The chief's brow furrowed more, and he shook his head. "Well, can you at least see Ms. Howard out?" Without waiting for a response, Archer ducked back inside his office and closed the door, leaving Chad alone with Tessa.

He glanced from the chief's closed door to the one next to his that belonged to Sergeant Terlecki. Chad had come upstairs to offer Kent a word of support, but instead he wrapped his fingers around Tessa's wrist and steered her toward the elevator.

"*Thanks a lot*," Tessa said with total insincerity as irritation— *not* his touch—heated her blood. She shook his hand off her arm. "If you hadn't come along, I would have talked him into signing up."

He chuckled as he reached for the Down button of the elevator. "I don't think so."

"Why?" Pride lifted her chin. "I'm good at my job."

The elevator must have been waiting because the doors slid open instantly. His hand touched the small of her back now, guiding her into the empty car. "I don't doubt that you're quite the saleswoman," he said.

Somehow she felt insulted rather than complimented. "What are you implying?"

"Just that you're not above using your wiles to get what you want—a contract—" he arched a dark brow "—or a free pass on a ticket."

"Well, *you* didn't give me a free pass." Which didn't say much for her wiles since he hadn't been a bit interested then—or now.

"And the judge didn't give you a free pass, either," the lieutenant said. "Despite your recent attempt to sweet-talk him."

Heat rushed to Tessa's face. "Uh…"

"The judge e-mailed to warn me that you're trying to get out of the academy," Chad said, his voice sharp with disapproval. "Interesting that you weren't above using your participation to score points with the chief, though."

"I *am* participating," she said. Because she hadn't been able to talk the judge into changing her punishment. She'd even offered to pick up trash along the highway instead.

"But not of your own free will, like you wanted the chief to believe."

"What are you—the sales spiel police? Do you take exception to everything I do or say?"

"Only when it's not the entire truth."

"You sound like you're my father," she said, not that she had a lot of experience with what a father sounded like. Hers hadn't stuck around long; he hadn't even waited for her to be born. But then, given her mother's taste in men, that might have been a good thing; some of her siblings' dads had stuck around too long.

A muscle twitched in his cheek. "I'm not old enough to be your father."

"No, but you're stuffy enough."

"I'm not *stuffy*," he protested. Clearly she'd struck a nerve.

"Oh, Lieutenant…" She emitted a pitying sigh. "You have no idea how stuffy you are."

"Just because I didn't let you flirt your way out a ticket?" he asked. "Flirting has surely failed you before, like it just did with the chief."

"You think I was flirting with the chief?" she asked, thoroughly insulted now. Not that the chief wasn't a good-looking man. Despite his having the highest position in the department, he probably wasn't quite old enough to be her father, either.

"You were wasting your time," he said, as he released a pitying sigh of his own. "The chief just lost his wife last year. He's too loyal a man to notice another woman yet. Even you."

"Even *me?*" He may not have meant that as a compliment, but Tessa took it as such.

Chad squeezed his eyes shut as if he regretted what he'd revealed. Then he admitted, "Even you. You know what you look like."

She smiled. "My mama passed on good genes." For physical appearance. For picking men, she had also passed on her lousy judgment genes, regrettably. Tessa had dated too many losers to be flattered by any man, yet the lieutenant wasn't trying to flatter her. If anything, he was still insulting her. Her smile widened. "I hadn't thought *you* noticed what I look like, Lieutenant."

The elevator bell dinged as it reached the lobby, but Tessa reached out and pressed the door button, holding them closed.

"Your flirting doesn't affect me any more than it did the chief," Michalski assured her.

"I wasn't flirting with the chief," she pressed. "You'd *know* if I was flirting."

"I would," he agreed—too easily—then added, "but I don't think you do. It's probably just second nature to you, kind of like your speeding."

"I know when I flirt."

Unfortunately, so did he. Since her traffic stop, he hadn't been able to forget the way she'd trailed her fingers over his and leaned in through her open SUV window, her breath nearly tickling his ear. His pulse quickened at the memory and at the reality of being alone with her. The elevator dinged again as someone probably stood on the other side of the doors, pressing the Up or Down button. But Tessa held the Close button again, trapping them inside the small car.

He could have easily brushed aside her hand and opened the doors, but he leaned against the wall of the elevator and wrapped his hands around the brass railing to prevent himself from pulling her into his arms.

"I don't think you do know when you're flirting," he argued with her arbitrarily. Was he wanting to rile her as much as she had tried to rile him with her "stuffy" insult? "I think you act just as recklessly with your…wiles as you do your driving."

"Recklessly?"

"Some day you might flirt with the wrong man," he warned her, "one who doesn't understand that you're not really aware of what you're doing."

"I know when I flirt," she repeated, jabbing the Close button again. Then she crossed the small space separating them, swaying her hips with just a couple of steps. She didn't stop until her body touched his. Then she lifted her chin, staring up at him, her blue eyes wide and bright.

"Lieutenant…" she murmured as her fingers trailed up his chest to tap his badge.

He knew she was playing with him, teasing the stuffy police officer and trying to prove her point. But his heart beat hard beneath his vest. "Tessa…"

She bit her full bottom lip and then swiped the tip of her tongue across it, moistening her mouth. Her lips parted and she breathed the word, "Yes…"

He hadn't realized he'd asked a question. To what was she giving permission—for him to kiss her? He leaned forward…

just as the elevator dinged again. Without her finger on the button, the doors slid open to a trio of rookie officers standing in the lobby. Heat climbed to Chad's face from where it had pooled lower in his body, where Tessa's curvy body brushed his.

One officer whistled.

One whispered, "Oh, man…"

And the third spoke coherently, "Lieutenant, we didn't want to be late for roll call. But we'll take the stairs."

"Sorry," muttered the whistler as they whirled away from the elevator.

The rookies weren't going to be the only ones late for roll call. Chad closed his eyes and groaned.

Tessa's body, lush and soft, settled fully against his. He swallowed another groan, fighting to keep his body from reacting to her closeness. He dragged in a breath, but it smelled of her—some light floral scent and fruity shampoo. He gripped the brass railing so hard he nearly snapped it free of the elevator wall. But he wouldn't reach for her. Even though his body hardened to the point of pain, he couldn't give in to temptation.

Her lips brushed his throat as she murmured, "Now that's flirting."

Feeling her gaze on his face, Chad kept his eyes closed. He couldn't see her this close and not lean down those few inches to press his mouth across hers, to find out if she tasted as sweet and naughty as she smelled.

She eased away and added, "And no matter what you claim, my flirting affects you."

He opened his eyes just in time to watch her hips sway as she sashayed out of the elevator and walked across the lobby. She was right. *She* affected him. And he couldn't have that— he couldn't have *her.*

Chapter Three

Flirting with Lieutenant Michalski had been a bad idea. She had proved him right; she *had* acted recklessly. Now, after flirting shamelessly with him, she had to see him again at the CPA class. Her face warmed as she walked into class—late. She ducked her head, hoping not to draw attention to her entrance.

But Amy, the college girl, called out, "I saved your seat!" and waved her to the table at the front of the room.

"You almost missed us, Ms. Howard," Lieutenant O'Donnell remarked from where he leaned against the officers' table. "We were just about to leave for our tour of the department."

Great, if she had been a little later, she could have justified leaving to the judge, if she had walked into an empty room. He would have had to let her miss this class.

"We'll break into smaller groups to get into elevators," O'Donnell continued. "We have sixteen citizens, now that Ms. Howard has joined us." While Michalski, seated behind the officers' table, stared at her in disapproval, O'Donnell winked at her. "There will be an officer with each group, so don't worry about getting lost. And feel free to leave your academy binder and personal stuff in the room."

Chairs creaked and voices rose in conversation and excitement over the tour. Tessa glanced down at the briefcase she had propped next to her chair. While the leather bag was heavy, it was also too important for her to risk leaving behind.

"It'll be safe," a deep voice assured her.

She lifted her gaze to Chad's handsome face. Along with those gold-flecked green eyes, he had chiseled features. She sighed, disgusted that such good looks were wasted on a man with such an uptight personality. To silently challenge his claim, she raised a brow.

"You're in a police department," he reminded her.

"But *someone* pointed out last week how dangerous this area is at night."

"*Outside*," he explained. "On the streets. You're safe in here."

The memory of the two of them in the elevator—her body pressed against his long, lean frame—passed through her mind. She shook her head. She wasn't safe in here—not with him. But she left her briefcase beside her chair and turned to leave the room, which had already emptied. He followed her as she walked down the hall to the elevators.

"You were late again," he remarked disapprovingly.

"I was in the building."

"Flirting with the chief again?"

She ignored his snarky comment, too filled with triumph and pride to be offended. "I was signing up the Lakewood PD as a client."

Michalski grimaced with disgust. "I really thought the chief was immune to a woman's charms."

"I'm sure he is," she agreed. "But, as I mentioned before, I wasn't flirting. I offered the best service available. The fastest T1 line, reliable, accessible—"

He chuckled. "The chief gave you the account. You can stop selling now."

"No, I can't." She had too many bills at home, too many responsibilities. "Not in this business." She quickened her pace to join the rest of the class by the elevators; she did not want to wind up alone with Chad again.

"Don't you ever slow down?" he asked as he lengthened his stride to match hers. Even in those ridiculously high heels, the woman moved as quickly as she talked. And as she drove. He sighed. "I guess I know the answer to that." She wasn't ever going to slow down, no matter what she learned in the class.

"Lieutenant, are you going to be our guide?" Amy asked as she batted her lashes at Chad.

Her flirting didn't affect him like Tessa's. Hell, Tessa got under his skin even when she wasn't flirting. Like now, when she was all but ignoring him.

But wearing a bright red suit, with her blond hair swinging around her shoulders, she was impossible to ignore. When the elevator arrived, he stepped back, allowing the members of his group to file in first. Memories of the last time he'd shared an elevator with Tessa flashed through his mind, but he pushed them away and stepped inside the crowded car.

His group consisted of the overly enthusiastic college girl, an older Neighborhood Watch captain, Tessa and the grand-daughter of the owner of the Lighthouse Bar and Grille. The Lighthouse was where most of the police department hung out before and after shifts for great food and conversation with people who actually understood the job.

During the tour, he did his best to keep his mind off Tessa. He focused instead on explaining the workings of the department, showing the 911-command room, the locker room, the gym and the roll-call room. When he brought them to the office floor, which was all but deserted this late in the evening, he stepped back. "Do you want to handle this area, Ms. Howard? You've been up here a few times."

Her blue eyes narrowed in a glare. "That's fine. I'm sure everyone—" she glanced at Amy "—would rather listen to you."

"Lieutenant, do you have an office up here?" Amy asked. "I'd love to see where you work when you're not out in your patrol car."

"I just use a desk in the roll-call room, which you already saw," Chad replied, with none of the charm Paddy had probably intended his tour guides to exhibit. But the girl's attention unsettled Chad. While he wasn't old enough to be her father, he felt old in comparison to her.

She was still in college although she acted younger than most of the kids he taught in the police academy at Lakewood U. She brought up memories of *his* crazy college days—playing hockey, frat parties, staying up all night to finish papers that should have been done earlier and would have been done earlier if he hadn't spent all his time with Luanne. Too bad he hadn't had more free time…

Fighting against the pressure building in his chest, he drew in a deep breath. He didn't know why Amy had made him think of his late wife—the young girl was nothing like Luanne. Strangely, Tessa reminded him the most of Luanne, even though the two women looked nothing alike.

"Can we go back down to the weight room?" Amy asked, sticking close as he continued to show his group around the office floor. "You must use that room a lot, Lieutenant."

Someone snorted over the girl's flirting, probably Tessa. The snort turned into a chuckle as he quickened his step to gain some distance from the girl.

"We need to get back to the conference room now," he said, herding the group toward the elevator. "Lieutenant O'Donnell is going to show some tapes," he said as they waited for the car, "that'll give you some insight into what a day in the life of an officer is like. Then you'll have some idea of what to expect on your ride-along."

As the elevator dinged and its doors slid open, Chad expelled a small breath of relief. He was so *not* tour-guide material. He owed Paddy for roping him into the job.

"Can I do my ride-along with you?" Amy asked, squeezing next to him in the elevator.

"Uh, Lieutenant O'Donnell hands out the assignments, so it's not up to me."

"Do we have to do the ride-along?" Tessa asked, speaking up from the other side of the elevator, which was probably as far from him as she'd been able to get without taking the stairs.

"For *voluntary* members of the academy, it's voluntary," he said and swallowed a chuckle over the anger that flashed through her blue eyes.

"Then can we put in a request for who we don't want to do our ride-along with?" she asked with a sassy smile.

"You can try." He fully intended to tell Paddy that Tessa was the last citizen he'd like to be paired with. As Amy shifted closer, he made a mental note to add her as the second to last.

TRY? TESSA INTENDED to get out of the ride-along entirely. She hadn't agreed to that when she had agreed to enroll in the CPA.

"Are you mad at me?" Amy asked her as they took their seats in the conference room.

"What?"

"For flirting with Lieutenant Michalski," she explained. "Are you and he…"

"No," Tessa assured her. "Not at all."

"Good."

"So you decided he wasn't too old for you after all?" Tessa said, intending her comment as teasing, but couldn't help that a little bitterness had crept into her voice. But she wasn't jealous—not at *all*.

Amy shrugged. "He is, but he sure is yummy. And I know there's something going on with Sergeant Terlecki and Erin—"

"No, there isn't," Erin Powell denied hotly as she slid into the chair on the other side of Tessa. "There's *nothing* going on between me and the sergeant."

"Sure," Amy humored her.

The girl obviously didn't read the *Chronicle*, or she would have realized the only thing going on between Terlecki and Erin was mutual hatred. Yet the reporter had been part of his group for the tour…

Tessa turned and studied the other woman. "What *is* that old saying about love and hate?"

Erin shook her head and sighed. "Not you, too." She leaned closer and whispered. "Not every female is here to land a lawman, you know."

Tessa chuckled. "Hey, you don't have to tell me. I don't even have time for this *class,* let alone a *man.*"

"I have time for only one man," Erin shared.

Tessa glanced toward the officers' table, at the handsome blond sergeant and then she turned back to Erin with a raised brow.

"Not *him*," she repeated, a scowl marring her smooth forehead. The furrows cleared when she smiled and explained, "My little man is only three and a half feet tall."

"You have a son?" Tessa would have guessed Erin was not much older than Amy, but then age had nothing to do with parenting. Her mother had gotten pregnant with Tessa before finishing high school.

"Nephew," Erin said, "but he's my responsibility right now."

Tessa understood those kinds of responsibilities, the ones that really belonged to someone else but had become yours. "I have—"

"Please turn your attention to the overhead where we'll be playing tapes of some traffic stops," Lieutenant O'Donnell directed, interrupting Tessa before she could share the number and ages of her siblings.

The watch commander nodded and someone flipped off the lights. "This will give you an idea of the day in a life of a patrol officer and what some of you will have to look forward to on your ride-alongs. This shows you how we don't know what to expect with even the most routine of traffic stops, so each of you will need to stay in the cruiser until your officer indicates you can leave the vehicle. Your safety, the public's safety and our officers' safety are of utmost importance to the Lakewood PD."

Next to her, Erin snorted in derision.

Tessa closed her eyes. Because she was *not* a police groupie, nor participating out of any interest in law enforcement, she intended to recharge from her long day of running from sales call to sales call to high school to middle school to elementary school, dropping off and picking up kids and taking forgotten lunches or lunch money or books or homework...

But then a familiar deep voice requesting, "License and registration, please," drew her attention to the screen. Lieutenant Michalski stood next to an equally familiar black SUV.

She cringed and slumped in her chair as a woman coyly remarked, "Good afternoon, Officer. I must have a taillight out, right? How sweet of you to stop and inform me."

Yet the SUV's lights burned red even in the fuzzy video footage.

"Both lights are working, ma'am."

"Then I can't imagine *why* you stopped me."

"You were speeding," he said, lifting his hand toward her open window. "License and registration."

As she passed them over, her hand lingered on his, her index finger stroking his skin. "I can give you my card, too, if you'd like my phone number."

Chuckles emanated from the darkness, and Amy nudged her with an elbow. "That's you!" Then in a louder voice, she exclaimed, "That's Tessa!"

Tessa's face burned with humiliation, but her screen image knew no such shame. "Officer…*Lieutenant* Michalski," she murmured as she leaned through the open window, reading the thin brass pin with his name above his badge. Then she blinked up at him. "I can't imagine why you think I was speeding…"

"Because you were," he stated unequivocally, with no discernible reaction to her flirting, the dark glasses hiding his eyes. "I'll be right back with your ticket."

"Wait!" But he walked away from her in the video. If only that had been the last she'd seen of him…

Chad clicked off the computer, freezing the frame on his handsome face as he walked back toward his car. Even with the low quality of the footage, the muscle twitching in his cheek was visible as he clenched his jaw.

"That was the classic," he said, having taken over for the watch commander, "flirt-your-way-out-of-a-ticket reaction—"

"Starring CPA member Tessa Howard," one of the other participants said, laughing. The kid, who had shared in the introductions last week that he was in the criminal justice program at Lakewood University, acted as if Tessa had starred in another kind of video.

"So did you give her the ticket?" one of Chad's fellow officers asked as he chuckled, too.

"Why do you think I'm here?" Tessa replied for him, lifting her palms and sighing with resignation.

"So the flirting didn't work?" Amy asked, her eyes wide with disappointment.

Tessa shook her head. "Not with the lieutenant."

"But you gave a valiant effort," someone praised her—the older woman who had talked her husband into joining the program for "thrills." Bernice, or Bernie as she preferred, began to clap, and the other CPA members joined in the applause.

Tessa stood up and bowed, as if she had just performed a play. In a way she had, a very public play for the lieutenant's interest.

As if he hadn't noticed her sassy response, Chad continued speaking, "It's an officer's duty to uphold the law and treat all violators fairly."

"No matter how pretty they are," Terlecki interjected, but his focus was on Erin, not Tessa.

"So my ugly mug won't cause me to get more tickets?" Bernie's husband, Jimmy, asked from where he sat next to his wife in the middle of the room.

"You're just as handsome as the day I married you," Bernie dutifully assured him.

"Then what the hell were *you* thinking thirty-nine years ago?" he joked.

Relieved the attention had shifted from her, Tessa released a breath. Then she risked a glance toward Chad and found his gaze on her. Did he care that he had embarrassed her? Or had that been his intention when he'd included the footage of her traffic stop? As in the video, his face was unreadable.

"Let's turn back to the screen, folks," he directed every-one. "We have a few more examples we'd like you to see." As the next video flickered across the screen, he warned, "If anyone finds foul language offensive, you may want to plug your ears…"

The few laughs that emanated from the CPA participants died out as the young female officer on the screen walked up to the open window of the car she had pulled over. The driver hurled insults and curses at the officer, who didn't even flinch. But Tessa tensed, fisting her hands at her sides as she took ex-ception to the chauvinistic remarks.

When the young officer asked the man to step out of his vehicle, the driver gunned the engine and took off. A gasp spilled from Tessa's lips, which others echoed.

"He was later apprehended," Chad assured them, "with a blood alcohol level well over the legal limit. But he filed a com-plaint against the department and that officer for harassment."

A few curses of outrage emanated from the CPA participants.

"So Tessa was the honey and that guy was the vinegar," Jimmy said.

Lieutenant Michalski ignored his remark, of course, and played the next video. An officer stood beside another vehicle. The audio had been turned down so Tessa couldn't hear what either the officer or the driver said. But then metal crashed against metal, the sickening crunch reverberating in the quiet conference room.

Tessa jumped, startled by the noise and horrified by what she saw on the large screen. A truck hit first the police car, so that the camera shook but kept recording the image of the officer's own vehicle hitting him.

Even though he didn't make a sound, Chad drew her at-tention. In the flickering glow from the screen, his face was eerily pale, his green eyes dark and haunted. Sweat beaded on his upper lip and his brow. She rose a few inches from her chair, compelled to go to him, to see if he was all right, but then he spoke.

"Officer Jackson's injuries were surprisingly minor," he said. "A broken leg and bruised ribs. He recovered quickly to return to work."

Tessa settled back on to her chair, but remained on edge, unsettled by her response to Chad's reaction to the tape. She didn't understand it, either. Since Officer Jackson hadn't been seriously injured, why had Chad tensed so much?

"And this next officer also survived," he told them in advance of running the tape.

Yet the warning wasn't quite enough to prepare them for what they saw. On the big screen an officer walked up to a vehicle, and before he approached the driver's side, someone clad in a dark hoodie and baggy jeans jumped out the van's back door and started shooting. Due to the camera angle, it appeared as though the bullets were coming straight out of the screen toward the viewers.

The class uttered gasps of horror—except for Amy who screamed. Tessa held her breath, horrified by the images she'd just seen.

"Officer Bowers's vest and his quick thinking saved his life," Chad assured them.

While these officers had survived, Tessa knew there were officers who hadn't been as fortunate, based on the daily reports on the evening news. And she remembered *those* images, but in her mind, each of those fallen officers was Chad. She squeezed her eyes shut to ease the sting of tears.

When the lights flipped back on, silence hung heavy in the room—everyone was as stunned as she was. Then someone, maybe the kid now rethinking his college major, asked, "Why do you do it?"

"Because it's our job," Sergeant Terlecki answered, but all the officers nodded their agreement.

Tessa shivered at how matter-of-factly they faced the potential of danger every day.

"In the back of your binders is a release form and sign-up sheet for ride-alongs," Lieutenant O'Donnell said. "Consider this footage when you make your decision for whether or not to participate. Then pick a few dates that'll work for you. Our shifts are twelve hours long."

"Twelve hours?" Jimmy gasped.

"You won't have to stay for the whole twelve-hour tour," the watch commander assured him. "The officer you're assigned would be happy to bring you back early."

"That's no fun," Bernie said, patting her nervous husband's hand. "You have to stay for the whole shift so you don't miss anything exciting."

"It's not always exciting," O'Donnell warned her. "But this is a great opportunity for you to experience, firsthand, a day in the life of an officer."

A day in Chad's life. It was not all flirting girls. It was uncertainty and danger. That bothered Tessa—and it bothered her more that it bothered her. That *he* bothered her.

KENT SLAPPED Chad on the back as they filed out of the empty conference room just ahead of Paddy, who shut off the lights. "Way to go, man, on standing firm with Blondie."

"What?"

"The video feed of your traffic stop with the hot blonde," Kent explained as if Chad didn't know exactly about what and whom his fellow officer spoke.

He shrugged. "Hey, you've been there." Just not since he'd taken a bullet for the chief three years ago, earning his nickname and desk job because of his inoperable injury.

"And I've let a few go with a warning," Kent admitted, "especially when they turn on the waterworks."

Paddy clicked his tongue in disapproval. "Makes you wonder how Bullet holds the department's arrest record, huh?"

"But Junior holds the citation record," Kent reminded them. "He never lets anyone off with a warning."

Luanne hadn't listened to all his warnings; now she was dead. He'd failed her. He didn't want to fail anyone else. That was why he'd included the footage of not just Tessa's traffic stop but of Officer Jackson's accident, too. That sound of metal crunching metal rang yet in his ears, reminding him again of Luanne's accident. He tried to block it out as his stomach lurched.

Had Tessa understood that speeding could have killed a police officer? That if she didn't slow down and focus on her driving instead of on her cell phone, she could have another accident, one in which more than a mailbox got hurt?

He cleared his throat and asked Paddy, "Did Ms. Howard turn in her sign-up sheet?"

Paddy shook his head. "I don't think she's interested in a ride-along."

"She needs to do it," Chad insisted. "The whole purpose of her being in the program is so she'll stop speeding." Or else he wouldn't have suggested the CPA as an alternative for her ticket.

Paddy nodded. "Sure, I'll tell her the ride-along is mandatory."

"Thanks."

"He's just saying that because he wants to be the one to drive her around," Kent teased.

"Hell, no!" he protested, not liking the thought of a twelve-hour shift with Tessa sitting beside him—too close, too damn beautiful and sexy.

His fellow officers laughed at his vehemence.

"C'mon," Kent persisted as they waited for the elevator. "We saw your face on that tape when you were walking back to your car. You might have given her the ticket, but she got to you."

And that was why he couldn't be assigned to her. She would distract him from his job, which was all he wanted in his life now and all he'd ever allow himself to care about again.

"Yeah," he agreed with his friends, "she got to me. She *annoyed* me."

"She could *annoy* me anytime," Kent remarked with an appreciative whistle.

Chad sucked in a quick breath at a stab in his ribs. It was as if his friend had shoved a knife in his back. He couldn't be jealous. He wasn't interested in Tessa Howard, but somehow he found himself reminding Kent of his reporter. "You have your own *annoyance*."

The other man uttered a curse then a heavy sigh. "You guys going to the 'house?" he asked, referring to the Lighthouse Bar and Grille, which boasted the best burgers in Lakewood.

Chad shook his head. "I'm finishing up Reynolds's shift in a couple of hours. He could only work a half tonight. He's gotta get some sleep before he goes to his kid's show-and-tell tomorrow." Chad was used to filling in for the guys who had families, and he didn't mind working the extra hours because they usually helped him forget that he didn't have one.

"I'll buy you a burger before you go on duty," Paddy offered. "I appreciate your help with the program."

"I'm almost done," Chad reminded his friend and himself.

He was almost done seeing Tessa Howard. "I only need to explain the pursuit policy and demonstrate the traffic stop procedure, and my obligation to the program is fulfilled."

Paddy shook his head. "I need you to do a ride-along, too, Junior. I need you to do *her* ride-along."

Chapter Four

"You're sure everything's all right?" Tessa asked Audrey, the cell phone pressed to one ear while she plugged a finger into her other ear to block out the noise of the crowded bar.

"Everyone's sleeping," Audrey murmured, then groggily griped, "At least we were until *you* called."

"The younger kids could sleep through an earthquake," Tessa reminded her teenage sister. But maybe she shouldn't have; she wouldn't put it pass Kevin and Audrey to throw a party on one of the nights she was at the class.

Thirteen more weeks. Only thirteen more weeks, she silently chanted. "Okay then, go back to sleep. I'll be home in a little bit."

"I'll be sleeping—unless you wake me up again," Audrey grumbled as she hung up the phone.

"I love you, too," Tessa muttered to the dial tone before she clicked shut her phone and dropped it into her briefcase.

"Thanks for coming tonight," Erin Powell said as she joined Tessa in the game area of the bar/restaurant. "It's good to have at least one friendly face here. Since I'm not exactly welcome."

"Really?" Tessa pointed toward the dartboard with a

blown-up picture of Erin's face tacked to it. Several holes pierced the brunette's pretty smile and the bridge of her delicate nose. "I never would have guessed."

"Maybe you shouldn't be seen with me," the reporter remarked.

Tessa shrugged. "I already have the Lakewood Police Department's account." She linked arms with the other woman. "So tell me who the *Chronicle* uses for their tele-communications provider…"

Erin laughed. "You have the perfect personality for sales." Her smile grew wistful. "Everyone likes you."

As Tessa noticed a familiar set of broad shoulders wedged in among those gathered around the bar, she shook her head. "Not everyone."

"You actually don't seem to like him much, either," Erin said, following her gaze to Chad's back.

"True."

"Because he showed the video of your traffic stop?"

"I didn't like him even before that," Tessa admitted.

"You're still mad he gave you the ticket?" Erin asked. "Were you really not speeding?"

A grin tugged at Tessa's mouth. "No, I was *really* speeding."

"Then why are you mad?"

"It's just his attitude, you know?" Her frustration with Lieutenant Michalski bubbled over. "That whole superior, he's-never-done-anything-wrong attitude of his drives me crazy."

"That must be part of their job training," Erin remarked as she glanced at the blond-haired guy who sat at the long table with several members of the citizens' police academy. As the group hung onto Terlecki's every word, laughing, Erin's brow furrowed, but she betrayed no other emotion. Apparently she released her frustration only at her computer.

"Why don't you find us a couple of seats at the table, and I'll grab us a couple of drinks?" Tessa offered.

"You don't have to do that…"

"I just got a big contract today," Tessa reminded her. "Plus, I need to butter you up so you'll put in a good word for me at the *Chronicle*."

Erin chuckled. "Okay, but just a club soda for me. My mom's watching Jason, and…well…you know how moms are…"

Not really. Tessa only knew *her* mother, and in comparison to her friends' mothers, she'd realized long ago that hers wasn't exactly the norm—at least not for the conservative area of Lakewood where she'd grown up.

"Two club sodas," Tessa agreed, then headed toward the bar.

She probably could have joined Erin at the table and waited for the waitress to come by again for their drink order. Instead, she pressed in close to one particular man seated at the bar. Over his shoulder she noted the drink in front of him. Beads of condensation rolled down the glass filled with ice and amber liquid and pooled in a circle on the polished surface of the bar. Chad closed his big hand around the glass, lifted it to his lips and took a deep gulp. His throat moved as he swallowed.

After the footage he'd shown—not of her futile flirting—but of the other traffic stops—he probably needed a drink. Yet disappointment tugged at her. While she had suspected Chad had some sorrows, she hadn't expected him to be the type to drown them.

She leaned in closer, her lips nearly brushing his ear as she accused, "Hypocrite."

Chad's skin tingled from the warmth of her breath. "Hypocrite? I'd expected you to call me a name or two because I showed the tape of your stop, but I didn't see that one coming. I'm not sure what I did to earn it."

She tapped his glass, tracing her fingertip around its rim. "You're drinking."

He could have corrected her misconception, but instead he asked, "Isn't that why you're here? To celebrate your new contract?"

He gestured toward the young bartender, Brigitte Kowalczek, who was also a member of the CPA, then turned back to Tessa. "Champagne?"

Tessa leaned over the bar, the side of her full breast rubbing against his arm. "Two club sodas, please, Brigitte," she requested as she pulled her wallet from her ever-present briefcase.

He closed his hand over hers. "I've got it." He gestured for the bartender to include the drinks on his bill. "So you're not much for celebrating?"

"I'm not much for drinking," she shared, and a hint of pain darkened her blue eyes, making him realize Tessa Howard went much deeper than her beautiful surface. She tapped his glass. "Not like you."

He glanced at his watch. "I'm taking over someone's shift in an hour."

"And you're drinking? Who's really the reckless one of the two of us?" Her full lips twisted with derision. "Hypocrite."

"While you're waiting for your drink, take a sip of mine," he offered, lifting the rim to her lips.

Tessa wrinkled her nose as if the bubbles tickled it. A ridiculous urge came over him to tickle her, to run his fingers up her ribs and see if she would squirm as she'd made him squirm in the elevator the other day. Fortunately the rookies feared him enough that they had not spread around the reason why Chad had been late for roll call that night.

She had also cost him a few nights' sleep. He lay awake thinking of her, worrying about her and worrying about how she made him feel—that she had *made* him feel again. He much preferred the numbness.

No, he wouldn't touch her because he would be the one who'd wind up squirming again, not her.

She licked her lips and commented, "It's ginger ale."

He nodded. "Just ginger ale."

"It doesn't matter what you drink," she said. "You're still the reckless one."

"How's that?" he asked, unable to follow her logic, such as it was.

"I *watched* all those tapes," she reminded him. "I know how dangerous your job is."

"But that doesn't make me reckless," he pointed out. "In fact, that makes me more cautious and careful. A man doesn't live long in my profession if he's reckless."

"So why did you decide to be a police officer?" she asked as if she was really interested in his answer.

Since she'd already called him a hypocrite, Chad decided to tell her the truth. "So I could speed without breaking the law."

"Funny," she said. "You're mocking me."

"Actually, I'm not. I was pretty crazy in high school and college," he admitted. "Then *I* grew up."

"Then you got stuffy," she said, reminding him of their encounter in the elevator.

Heat flashed through his body, but he ignored it. He shook his head. "It didn't take me long on the job to understand how dangerously I'd been living."

"Don't you ever get tired of it?" she asked, tilting her head as she studied him.

He tried to focus on her words, not her face—not her lips. "Tired of my job?"

She shook her head, and a strand of blond hair brushed his jaw. "No, of being so damned perfect. Don't you get tired of it?"

He snorted in surprise. The last thing he'd expected from her was a compliment, however undeserved. "I'm not perfect."

She blew out a breath. "Really? You don't think so?"

He knew he wasn't. If he were perfect, his wife would still be alive. He would have been able to make her act more cautiously and carefully. But like Tessa, Luanne had refused to slow down.

"Then if you don't think you're perfect," she challenged, "why the hell are you so sanctimonious all the time?"

He laughed, more comfortable with her insults than her praise. "First I'm a hypocrite. Now I'm sanctimonious. I don't think you're just mad about the class. I don't think you're even all that mad about my including the tape tonight because it certainly didn't embarrass you."

"Is that why you did it?" she asked. "You wanted to embarrass me?"

If he had, his plan had backfired. He'd embarrassed himself more than he had her because now Paddy and Bullet had some crazy idea that Chad was interested in her. Or maybe the rookies *had* talked…

"I was just proving a point," he said, "like you were in the elevator."

A smile curved her lips. "Ohh, you were trying to prove that my flirting didn't get to you. We're back to that?"

He shook his head, never more certain that including the video of her traffic stop had been a bad idea. Like bringing up the CPA to the traffic court judge.

She leaned close again, her lips brushing against his ear. "I was plastered against you in that elevator. I know exactly how much I got to you."

Her words and her breath were warm on his skin, bringing back the memory of her body warm and soft against his. He fought a groan, not wanting to give her the satisfaction.

She glanced down at his lap, then back to his face, her blue eyes brimming with amusement.

Chad ignored his physical reaction to her because he couldn't control it. He could, however, control his emotional one. "You can flirt all you want, Ms. Howard, I'm not going to fall for you."

"I don't want you to fall for me," she said, drawing back as if he'd slapped her. "I don't even like you."

"And it's not because of the ticket, or the class, or the tape," he said, returning to the thread of their conversation. "Why don't you like me?" he wondered.

"Because you're too perfect."

"HE'S NOT, you know," Brigitte commented as she collapsed onto the chair next to Tessa at the long table. The rush at the bar had subsided for the moment. And several of the CPA members had left, too: the teachers, who needed to get up early for class, the youth minister and Erin.

"What?" Tessa asked.

"Lieutenant Michalski, he's not too perfect."

At least a half hour had passed—Chad had even left the bar—since Tessa had made the comment, but still she regretted saying what she had. Usually she would argue that she was not reckless, but with him she was, acting and talking without thinking through the consequences.

"It doesn't matter if he has a few flaws," she said although she doubted her words. "He's still too perfect. And I don't trust perfect." *Perfect* built up your hopes that this guy was different, that he would stick around. Then when he took off like everyone else, it hurt that much more, crushing your hope.

"Nobody's perfect," Brigitte said. "He doesn't always drink ginger ale."

"So he does drink?" She'd been right. The guy did have some sorrows—sadness had glinted in his eyes like specks of gold. Instead of vindication at being right, sadness pulled at her, too.

The auburn-haired bartender nodded. "Not for a while, but he used to. When he did, he'd have Lieutenant O'Donnell drive him home, though."

"He'd get pretty messed up then?"

Brigitte nodded. "The guy has some demons, you know."

"Don't we all?" But what demons chased Lieutenant Michalski? "Did he ever tell you what was bothering him?"

Brigitte shrugged. "You know that whole bartender-as-confessor thing is a myth."

Tessa smiled. "My mom's a bartender—it's no myth with her. She has listened to a lot of confessions and sob stories over the years."

And usually Sandy had felt so sorry for the guy that she had wound up falling for him. *Poor, sweet, delusional Mom...*

Why couldn't she learn what Tessa had come to accept long ago—that no one could be trusted? That men didn't stick around. You could only rely on yourself. Sandy should have realized that because every guy had left her to raise her kids alone. Watching her mom fail again and again at love was what had wised up Tessa.

"I don't believe what guys tell me when they're sober," Brigitte shared. "I'm sure as hell not going to believe them when they're drinking."

Tessa smiled, recognizing a kindred spirit. "You and I are going to be good friends."

She couldn't remember the last time she'd had a friend. Since she'd always had younger siblings to help care for, she hadn't had much time for friends in school or community college. Because she couldn't hang out at the mall or go to the movies or party, her classmates had stopped asking her to do things with them. Now, at work, she had competitors, not friends.

Brigitte sighed. "I'm usually here, helping out Gramps." During the first class she had shared that her grandfather owned the Lighthouse. "You'll have to come by more often. I could use a friend."

"Me, too." Tessa squeezed the other woman's hand, then implored, "So friend to friend, tell me what the lieutenant's demons are."

Brigitte laughed. "Seriously, I don't know. But you might want to ask the other lieutenant."

"O'Donnell?" She glanced to where the watch commander sat at the bar, munching on a plate of cottage fries.

"He usually knew when Michalski would need a ride, like it was an anniversary or something."

An anniversary of a divorce? He didn't wear a ring, but there was something about him that suggested he'd been the marrying kind, once upon a time. Tessa mentally shook her head, doubting that he'd ever been crazy enough, despite his claims, to fall in love. He was too careful, too cautious to have probably ever risked his heart.

She glanced at her watch. "I'd rather stay and visit longer, but I need to get home." To see if she had a home left since the kids had had no *real* supervision tonight. "I'm just going to tell Lieutenant O'Donnell good night."

"Yeah, right, you're going to pump him for information," Brigitte said. She winked. "You and I are going to be good friends."

First Erin, now Brigitte—heck, even Amy—Tessa had never made so many friends.

"Hello, Ms. Howard," O'Donnell greeted her without even looking up from his plate. "Are you bringing me your sign-up sheet for the ride-along?"

"No. I don't need to do that."

"That's not what Lieutenant Michalski believes."

"I don't care what Lieutenant Michalski believes," she shot back, then winced at how childish she sounded. She definitely needed to spend less time with her adolescent siblings and more time with adults.

Her voice calmer, she explained, "A ride-along wasn't part of my agreement with the judge."

"It's part of the program," O'Donnell persisted, "so it's part of the agreement. Unless you want me to call the judge."

"No, really, that's all right," she backed down. The judge had already warned her to stop bothering him or he'd change his mind about waiving her ticket and license suspension. "I'll bring the release form to next week's class."

"That's good, Ms. Howard," O'Donnell said with a grin. "I'm sure Lieutenant Michalski will be happy to know that."

"Is that possible?" she wondered aloud.

"Is what possible?"

She drew in a breath, bracing herself to flat out ask the question that had haunted her for some time, even more since watching his reaction to the traffic accident. "Is Lieutenant Michalski capable of happiness?"

O'Donnell's brow furrowed. "That's a strange question to ask."

She sighed, releasing the breath she'd held. "Well, the lieutenant doesn't seem to be a very happy man."

O'Donnell nodded. "You're pretty intuitive."

"In sales you have to be." Or she wouldn't have gone from telemarketer to top field sales agent. And if she hadn't, she wouldn't have been able to pay the bills for which she'd assumed responsibility.

If only she were as intuitive in her personal life as she was her professional one...

"Do you have to be curious in sales?" O'Donnell asked.

"It's good to be interested in people."

"Are you interested in Chad?" he asked, his gaze intent on her face as if she were a suspect he was interrogating.

She stumbled back a step, startled by his question. "No—no, I don't know where you would have gotten that idea."

"You're asking if he's happy," O'Donnell reminded her. "That's a pretty personal question."

"Yeah, you're right," she agreed, angry with herself for caring. "That was too personal."

He lifted a brow as he asked her, "So you don't want to know the answer?"

She backed away from the bar. "No. You're right. I don't need to know anything else about Lieutenant Michalski."

"Are you sure about that?"

"Absolutely."

No man was as perfect as Michalski acted. She didn't have to know what his flaws were to be certain that the man had them. Even if he didn't, he would undoubtedly run the other way once he learned how many responsibilities she had, just like every other man in her life had.

"I don't need to know anything else about Lieutenant Michalski." Thirteen more weeks. That was all she had left of the citizens' police academy and of Chad Michalski. "Sorry I asked."

"I'm actually glad that you did, Ms. Howard," O'Donnell admitted. "Because your instincts are right. Chad hasn't been happy for a while."

She resisted the urge to press her hands to her ears to avoid hearing anything more. She was already acting more like one of her teenage siblings than herself around Chad, and she resented him for compelling her to act that way.

"I really don't need to know anything else," she insisted as regret filled her that she had ever asked.

"I think you do," O'Donnell said, as if she'd passed some kind of test she hadn't realized she'd taken. "I think you could make him happy, if you wanted."

"I don't want," Tessa said. "I—I really don't want…" *Chad Michalski*. If she actually had time for a romantic relationship right now, the disapproving lieutenant would be the last man to interest her. She didn't trust his seeming *perfection*, but she trusted *herself* even less around him. Something about him compelled her to act as reckless and impulsive as he accused her of being.

SHE WASN'T INTERESTED in him—not at all. She had only asked about him because he irritated her with his sanctimonious, superior attitude. He was cautious and careful.

And she wasn't?

As she tiptoed barefoot around her own house, checking for signs of partying and doing a bed check, she begged to differ. She was damn cautious and careful. A door creaked as she pushed it open and crept across the threshold. The light from the hall fell across Christopher's and Joey's beds. Christopher's leg dangled from the top bunk, his face buried in the pillow. Joey lay on his side, drooling onto his blue chenille security blanket.

First she pushed Christopher's leg beneath the bed railing and his blankets. Then she leaned over and pushed Joey's bangs back from his forehead and pressed a kiss to his soft skin. They were good kids. Same with the girls who she found tucked tidily into their beds.

Suzie, with her porcelain skin and dark hair, looked like one of the dolls the little girl collected and that stared down at her from the shelves James had built around the perimeter of the girls' room before he'd left for college. Audrey lay on her back, snoring too loudly and unevenly to have been feigning sleep. Tessa swallowed a giggle at the noise and pulled their door closed.

Then she padded quietly toward the back of the house and slid open the bifold doors to the family room where Kevin made his bed on the pullout couch. But the room was empty.

"Damn it." It was nearly midnight. Where could the kid be? What kind of trouble could he be getting into tonight?

She headed back toward the kitchen, grabbing her keys off the counter before she rushed out the door. Kevin had sneaked off too many times; she was finding him tonight—even if she had to turn Lakewood upside down to locate him.

She checked the parking lot of Lakewood High School, then drove around the lakeshore to see if Kevin might have been stupid enough to jump off the pier, which seemed to be some Lakewood rite of passage; however, most of the kids who did it wound up getting hurt or drowned. She breathed a sigh of relief to find no one on the pier.

After looking through the park, she still hadn't found her brother, but she had scared off a couple of other kids and some couples who had probably only intended to "couple" for one night. Face warm with embarrassment and with anger at her brother for sneaking out—again—she turned out of the park and headed home. She drove slowly in case she spied him on the sidewalk. Suddenly a siren rang out—just one sick-sounding wail. Then red and blue lights flashed in her rearview mirror.

"No, no, no…" she murmured as she pulled to the curb,

then turned toward the passenger seat, the *empty* passenger seat. She'd forgotten her briefcase, in which she always stowed her wallet—and her *license*. "No, no, no…"

"That's what I was thinking," Lieutenant Michalski said as he walked up to her open window—she'd had it down to call out for Kevin. "No, no, no, but I ran your plate as I was following you through the park and sure enough, it was you."

"Then you don't need to see my license and registration again," she said, almost relieved it was Chad who had pulled her over. Yet her heart still pounded hard as if she'd been running fast instead of driving slow. "And you can't say I was speeding."

"I know," he agreed with obvious surprise. "That's why I had to pull you over. I had to make sure it was really you behind the wheel and that someone hadn't stolen your vehicle."

"It's really me," she assured him, "so you can let me go now."

He wrapped his fingers around her doorframe and leaned through the window. "I'm not letting you go…"

Her heart sped up even more, definitely exceeding the limit.

"…until you tell me what's going on."

"I—I—uh…" She couldn't tell him about Kevin; it was one thing for him to be in trouble with her, another for her to get him in trouble with the police. Chad, who took that whole serve-and-protect thing so seriously, would insist on helping her look for Kevin. And although she didn't think her brother was stupid enough to be doing something illegal, she actually had no idea what he *was* doing. *Damn kid.* Why wouldn't he talk to her?

"You weren't out making sales calls this late," Chad said, glancing from her face to the interior of the vehicle, as if he worried that she'd been hijacked. "You don't even have your briefcase with you, and I wouldn't have believed you ever left home without it."

"I don't carry it with me everywhere."

"But you keep all your stuff in it," he said, his brow furrowing.

"Uh, not always," she stammered.

"Tessa?" He lifted his hand from the doorframe and brushed a fingertip along her jaw. "Where's your license?"

"You agreed I wasn't speeding," she reminded him, pulling back slightly so that his hand fell away from her face. She didn't want him touching her…because then she couldn't think.

He retreated from the window. "You can't drive without a license—it's the law."

"I have a license, and you know it," she said, her frustration with him building again.

"It has to be on your person any time you're behind the wheel of a vehicle."

"But that doesn't make sense," she argued. "You can check that thing that you checked my plate with—"

"My computer."

"Yeah, you can check and see that I have a license."

"You have to carry it with you when you're driving, Tessa," Mr. Perfect repeated. Then he reached through the window, the back of his hand brushing against her thigh as he unlocked and opened the door. "Step out of the vehicle."

Anger bubbled up inside her, stinging her eyes with tears she refused to shed. "Why? Are you going to arrest me now?"

"Tessa—"

She jumped down from the SUV, the asphalt scraping the soles of her bare feet. Then she planted her palms against the side of the vehicle and spread her legs. "So go ahead and frisk me!"

Chapter Five

Hell, yes! Standing with her feet wide apart, Tessa's skirt rode up her thighs, baring the entire long, lean length of them. Along with her shoes and briefcase, she'd also taken off her suit jacket, leaving her clad only in that short skirt and a lacy camisole. He swallowed to clear his throat before he told her, "You're being ridiculous."

"Are you afraid to touch me?" she asked. "I have no needles on me."

She must have been referring to the video of an officer getting stuck with a dirty needle while frisking someone. One of the vice cops had shown it after the break following Chad's presentation,

"That doesn't make you any less dangerous," he muttered.

Her hair swung across her back as she turned her head toward him. "You *are* afraid to touch me."

Hell, yes!

But just running a fingertip along the delicate line of her jaw had rattled him. Even though he didn't trust himself to touch her, he wrapped his fingers around her wrist and turned her around to face him. He would not let his attraction to her distract him from doing his job.

"Tell me what's going on," he urged.

"Nothing out of the ordinary," she said as she tugged her wrist free. "You're being a hard-ass, as usual."

Chad resisted the urge to grind his teeth again and strove for patience. "If you tell me what's going on, I can help you."

She gave an unladylike snort that stirred a strand of hair from her cheek. "You're the first guy who has ever offered to *help* me."

He studied her eyes because something about her tone suggested she wasn't giving one of her usual flip responses but a heartfelt admission. But he didn't want to be the one man who'd helped her—he didn't want any connection with her at all.

"It's my job," he explained, against the panic rising to press against his chest.

"Of course. That's all I am to you—a job. A duty." She snorted again. "Someone to serve and protect."

"Protect and serve," he automatically corrected, then he found himself asking, "Do you want me to be more?"

She shook her head vehemently now. "I don't want you to be *anything* to me."

He sucked in a breath, taken by surprise that her comment had jabbed his heart. No, not his heart. His pride. He didn't want her to be anything to him, either. While he'd dated occasionally over the past four years, he had never gone out with anyone who'd wanted more than he could give or who'd tempted him to give more than he was ready to. And, considering how much he still missed Luanne, he doubted he'd ever be ready—especially with someone who'd probably meet as tragic an end as Luanne had.

"C'mon, Tessa, tell me what's going on," he insisted, his voice growing louder with his impatience—and his concern. "You shouldn't be out driving around alone at night with no shoes—*no* license. It's too dangerous."

She tilted her chin and crossed her arms over her chest. "It's also none of your business."

He sighed. "God, you're stubborn." Maybe she'd been right earlier—that he was a hypocrite—because he knew a thing or ten about being stubborn himself.

"Add it to the list," she quipped.

"What list?"

"The one you're keeping of all my faults. You know," she insisted as if checking off items on a grocery list, "I'm reckless, careless, a lying flirt—"

"And stubborn," he added, grateful for the reminder of all the reasons she couldn't be anything to him. "Now tell me what's going on with you tonight."

She shrugged. "Nothing's going on."

He fought for patience and calm, lowering his voice to a level of reason and understanding. "You left your briefcase—" he glanced down at her polished toes "—and your shoes somewhere. You're out driving around late at night and not at your usual breakneck speed."

"So are you going to give me a ticket for driving *under* the limit?"

"I should give you a ticket for driving without a license. Or actually take you in."

She uttered a squeak of frustration. "But I *have* a license."

"For now, until you get one more ticket," he reminded her.

"Chad…"

His breath caught in his throat. She hadn't yet called him anything but lieutenant—to his face—and undoubtedly some other names behind his back. Her name on his lips had him imagining other things on her lips—like *his*.

She lifted her hand toward his chest, but pulled it back as if unwilling to flirt, which said a lot more than her silence since he figured flirting was second nature to her.

"I'm not going to give you a ticket," he admitted, surprising himself almost as much as her since her eyes widened with shock. "I *am* going to take you home."

"I can't leave my vehicle here," she argued. "I'll need it in the morning."

"Afraid you might miss a sales call?"

"Come on, Chad," she beseeched him, "I need it."

That was what worried him—that she wasn't done driving around alone at night. "Not going to try flirting?"

She shook her head. "*I* don't affect you, remember?"

If only that were true, he might actually sleep at night. The dispatcher's voice crackled through the radio on his belt. "Stolen silver 2006 Buick Rainier. Two occupants. Early twenties…"

He listened to the direction in which the stolen car was headed, but even though Tessa didn't say a word, she distracted him. While his job was to help all of Lakewood, he was most concerned about Tessa Howard right now. Too concerned. "I want to know what's going on with you," he persisted.

"It's nothing really," she assured him. "You have to respond to that, don't you?"

He didn't have to; there were other units on duty. He had trained all the officers in the department, and regularly re-trained them on the pursuit policy; they could evaluate the risk factors of the chase. But there were some rookies on duty, who might get caught up in the adrenaline and ignore when the risk got too high.

Hell, she was right. He had to go. "I'm going to let you off *this* time."

"I bet you won't show this tape in class," she murmured as he headed back to his cruiser.

He intended to erase this tape. "Go right home, Tessa," he warned her.

"Chad?"

He turned back. "Yes?"

"Thanks," she said, her voice soft. "For wanting to help—even if it's just your job."

"Tessa…"

"You have to go," she reminded him.

He had to go—he had to get away from her.

"Chad?" she called him again.

He lifted his gaze to hers, hopeful that she was going to share with him whatever had brought her rushing out in the middle of the night.

"Be careful," she said. As if she cared…

His chest muscles tightened with her concern. As if he cared…

TENSION NAGGED and pressure built behind Tessa's eyes, blurring her vision as she stumbled inside the house. Now she wasn't only worried about Kevin, she was worried about Chad, too. Until tonight—she glanced at her watch—last night, she hadn't considered how dangerous his job actually was. However, he was careful and cautious, she reminded herself.

Unlike Kevin. She dropped her keys onto the kitchen counter, which had been cleared since she'd come home the first time. One side of the white porcelain sink held drying dishes, the other soapy water. She dipped her fingers inside; it was still warm.

"Did you want me to leave you the dishes?" her mother asked as she walked into the kitchen from the hall. Her blue eyes glinted with amusement.

"No," Tessa said.

"You must have left in a hurry," Mom said, pointing toward Tessa's bare feet, then the briefcase she'd left next to the counter. "Did you forget something?"

Tessa sighed. "Just that Kevin can't be trusted. He's not home."

"He's home," her mother said. "He's sleeping so hard I just checked to see if he's alive."

"He won't be when I get my hands on him," she promised, even though some of her tension eased with the knowledge that he was home and safe, for the moment at least. "Curfew means nothing to that kid. Where the heck does he go every night?"

"He's a teenager," Sandy said dismissively. "You're young enough to remember what that's like."

Tessa hadn't felt young for a long while, but she sometimes wondered if her mother would ever grow up. With her bleached blond hair and youthful attire of low-waisted jeans and a tank top she'd probably borrowed from Audrey, she didn't look much older than Tessa—or Audrey, actually.

Sandy defended her son by saying, "At his age, a kid wants to hang out with his friends."

"He might *want* to," Tessa allowed, "but he has other responsibilities."

"Like you," Mom said with a sigh, "you never got to hang out with your friends, did you? I've always asked too much of you."

Tessa stepped closer to her mother to determine if the older woman had been drinking. Sandy Howard had had problems with alcohol on and off for years, but Tessa had believed—had hoped—she'd been *off* for a while, since she'd been pregnant with Joey. Tessa breathed deep, inhaling the scent of stale cigarettes and the floral perfume her mother always used to try to disguise what she called "eau de bar." "Mom, are you okay?"

"I'm fine, honey," Sandy assured her. "It's *you* I'm worried about."

"Worry about Kevin. I haven't seen any of these *friends* he's hanging out with," she said, her concern returning. "Have you?"

"No."

She sighed. "I'm going to quit the academy."

She would get a lawyer—not that she could afford one—if she had to, to keep her driver's license.

Despite not often having acted like a parent over the years, Sandy shook her head as if Tessa had asked her permission. "You can't."

"I can't leave Kevin and Audrey in charge of the younger kids. They can't be trusted." Most people in her life hadn't proven trustworthy. Like Sandy, who'd promised every time she brought a guy home that he was the one—Mr. Right who would take care of them and never leave them.

"This wasn't a good idea," her mother said.

"I know. But the judge decided—"

"No, I meant this," Sandy said, gesturing around the country kitchen. "Living together. You're twenty-seven, Tessa. You should have a place of your own."

"I have the walk-out level." With a separate entrance, bathroom and kitchenette, it was more or less her own apartment, yet she was still close enough to watch her siblings and make sure no one got into trouble. She hadn't done a very good job watching Kevin lately. Where did the boy go, and more importantly, what did he do?

"You need a life of your *own*," her mother explained.

"I have a life of my own."

"No, you're living *mine*," Sandy said, her voice breaking with emotion. "You're cleaning up my messes. It's not fair to you. I've made a lot of mistakes."

Although she hadn't smelled any alcohol on her mother's breath, Tessa asked, "Have you been drinking?"

"No. That was a mistake I won't repeat," Sandy insisted. "I'm seeing clearly now. I'm seeing *you* clearly now." She narrowed her eyes as she studied Tessa's face. "Something's going on with you."

"This class—" And Chad, but she knew better than to mention a man's name to her mother, who still held out for the romantic fantasy of happily-ever-after. "It's a pain in my—"

"It's good for you," her mother insisted with a maternal warmth and certainty that reminded Tessa of Nana Howard, her mother's mother, who had really raised Tessa. She and Sandy had lived with her grandmother until Nana had died when Tessa had been Audrey's age—just fourteen. She blinked back tears, still missing the woman and loving this side of her mother. Of course Mom, though often flighty and irresponsible, was always loveable.

"You need something in your life besides work and family," Sandy proclaimed. "Like Kevin, you need to hang out with your friends."

"I'm worried about Kevin."

"It's not your job to worry about him," Sandy pointed out. "It's *mine*." She sighed, and as if she really had channeled Nana Howard, she said, "It's time I assume responsibility for all my mistakes."

"It's not your fault," Tessa defended her mother with a smile. "You have lousy taste in men, Mom."

Sandy smiled, too. "Yes, but that's my problem, not yours."

"I think it could be my problem, too," Tessa admitted.

Frowning, Sandy touched her face. "Oh, honey…"

"I've never found a guy who wanted to stick around, either," she reminded her mother. Tessa was probably genetically disposed to have the same lousy judgment. None of the boyfriends she'd had had been any more stand-up than her father—or any of the kids' fathers—no matter how perfect any of them had seemed in the beginning of the relationship.

"But you haven't looked for a while," Sandy persisted, ever the optimist. "Maybe you'll meet a nice guy in this class."

Heat rushed to Tessa's face.

Sandy's eyes twinkled with delight. "Maybe you already have."

"I'm not there to meet men, Mom. That's Amy's job." She grinned as she thought of the police groupie. "She's this college girl who's determined to land herself a lawman."

Mom's dark brows arched. "You're getting to know other people?"

"Yes. Erin, she's a reporter for the *Chronicle*." And probably like Tessa, she was too busy to make much time for friendships. "And Brigitte—she tends bar for her grandfather at the Lighthouse."

"I've applied there before," Sandy admitted. "They're open twenty-four hours so I could maybe get a morning shift."

"I'll put in a word for you with Brigitte," Tessa offered.

"You don't need to do that. First Nana took care of me, and now you. You need to take care of yourself, Tessa. Make your own life," her mother urged her, then pulled her into a hug.

Tessa was too stunned to hug back. Who was this woman?

"You need to find yourself a man," Sandy added.

Now this was definitely her mother.

If Sandy met Chad, she would think he was Mr. Right, that he was as perfect as he seemed. Tessa knew better—no one was perfect…for her.

"HOW DO YOU LIKE your burger?" Chief Archer asked as he stood at the outdoor grill, his spatula held up to Chad like a weapon.

"Still medium," Chad replied from the corner of the brick patio that he paced. The chief knew damn well how he liked his burgers. They'd been getting together a couple times a month since the chief's wife had died the year before.

Frank Archer laughed. "Just trying to get you to talk. I don't think you've said two words since you got here."

Chad shrugged and grimaced as he rolled his shoulders, which had been tense since he'd pulled over Tessa Howard a few nights ago. "Just tired."

"You've been working some extra hours," the chief commented, always aware of what was happening in his department.

Chad nodded. "Yeah, just filling in where I'm needed."

"It's never enough," Archer said as he flipped a burger. Grease sputtered on the grill, and smoke wafted out, with the rich aroma of hickory and beef.

Chad's stomach growled; he couldn't remember the last time he'd eaten. Probably something he'd grabbed at the 'house or at the little pizza parlor around the corner from where he lived. "What's never enough?" he asked.

"Being needed at work," the chief explained. "It's not the same as being needed at home, as having someone special need you."

After all the years of his wife being so sick, Chad was surprised the older man wasn't somewhat relieved *not* to be needed—at least *that* way.

"Luanne never needed me," he admitted. "She was always so independent." Like Tessa Howard, whose refusal of his offer to help had been haunting him. What had brought her out so late at night, barefoot without her briefcase?

"Bonnie was old-fashioned," the chief shared with a wistful smile. "All she ever wanted was to be a wife and mother."

"You don't have kids," Chad blurted out before he remembered why.

"Bonnie wanted to wait until I was more established in my career."

That had been Chad's plan, too, but he knew now how quickly plans could change.

"By the time I was," Frank continued, "she'd gotten sick with her first occurrence."

Breast cancer. Bonnie Archer had found her first lump when she was still in her twenties. Then years later, cancer had come back in other areas. Despite a long, valiant fight, she'd lost her battle.

"In a way, though, I have kids," he insisted. "All of *you* officers are my kids."

Chad laughed. "You would have been what—twelve—when I was born?"

"Hey, I could have started young," Frank said with a grin. "Seriously, I do think of all you officers as my kids, and it bothers me when something's bothering one of you." He gestured with the spatula again, pinning down Chad. "What's bothering you?"

"Nothing," he lied, too used to keeping everything to himself since Luanne had died to share his feelings with anyone.

"Maybe I should have asked *who?*"

The *nobody* caught in his throat. No matter what she might have called him behind his back, or to his face, he couldn't call Tessa *nobody.*

"Kent mentioned a blonde," Frank persisted. "Was he referring to Ms. Howard?"

"Kent's got a big mouth."

"Not big enough for that reporter from the *Chronicle.*" The chief sighed. "The boy actually needs to talk more—about himself." He looked at Chad. "So do you. You've let me ramble on and pour out my heart for over a year now. It's your turn."

"I'm fine, really," Chad insisted. "It's been four years since *my* wife died."

"So are you over it?" Frank asked, his blue gaze soft with fatherly concern. "Are you over her?"

"How do you get over the love of your life?" Chad wondered.

"Fall for someone else," the chief suggested matter-of-factly as he slapped a burger on a sesame-seeded bun. He passed the plate to Chad, who accepted it with a slightly shaking hand.

"Fall for someone else?" Had the chief met someone, or were they still talking about Tessa and what everyone thought Chad was feeling for her?

"I know—easier said than done." Archer slapped another burger on a bun and, after shutting off the grill, carried his plate to the patio table to join Chad.

"Are you thinking about it?" he asked, nearly incredulous that the chief could move on so soon.

"Falling in love again?" The older man nodded as he tore open a bag of chips. "I miss it, you know. Being married. Having someone cook for me. Clean for me."

A smile tugged at Chad's mouth. "You don't want someone to need you, you want someone to take care of you," he teased.

"Maybe," Frank admitted. He settled back in his wicker chair and gazed at the elaborate gardens in brilliant bloom around the patio. "Or maybe I should just sell this place. It's too much work for me."

"Is that all it is?"

"Too many memories, too, I guess." He sighed. "Everywhere I look I see Bonnie. You sold your house—is that why?"

Chad pushed his plate away, his appetite gone. "I moved out because I didn't need it." The four-bedroom house with the big yard in which all his kids would have played. The baby's room Luanne had painted with a mural of cop cars and fire engines. Every colorful room had reflected her personality. "I work too much, so the condo suits me perfectly."

"But if you get married again—"

"I won't."

"Why not?"

"I knew when she died that I would never love anyone the way I loved her." Luanne had been his first love, the woman he'd planned on being his only love. He couldn't imagine falling for someone else. Yet Tessa's face sprang to his mind. "So it wouldn't be fair to anyone else or to *me* to try."

The older man pushed his plate away, too. "Falling in love again—definitely easier said than done…"

Chad sure as hell hoped so.

Chapter Six

Brakes screeched as a black SUV rounded the corner of the parking garage. Chad stepped in front of the CPA class that had gathered around a police cruiser and an unmarked car, but the black SUV pulled into a parking spot, and Tessa killed the engine—instead of killing him. He expelled a ragged breath, which thickened to a white cloud in the cold air. Despite being only late September, Lakewood was having one of its early freezes, which was typical for its northern Michigan lakeshore locale.

She was late. Again. Which she would no doubt use as her excuse for speeding in the parking garage.

"You were right," Paddy said with a chuckle. "She does need some driving-improvement courses." He leaned closer and pitched his voice lower than the chatter of the class. "Maybe you should give her *private* lessons."

Chad snorted. "Not damn likely that either of us would agree to that." Since she hadn't let him help her last week, he doubted she would appreciate any of his driving tips. That was fine with him. After his barbecue with the chief, he'd managed to focus again on the fact that he didn't want someone depending on him.

"This is the last class you need me for," he reminded Paddy and then himself. "The last time I have to see Tessa Howard."

Unless he pulled her over again. What the hell had been going on with her the other night, and why had she been so reluctant to tell him? Then again, why should she have? They weren't friends; they were nothing to each other. It needed to stay that way—for Chad's peace of mind.

She stepped down from her vehicle, her heel balancing precariously on her running board. She wore another short skirt, legs bare despite the chilly weather, and the sleeves of her jacket only reached her elbows. Hadn't she listened to the weather report? The damn woman was going to freeze.

He shook his head and sighed. She needed a keeper, however, he'd already proven he wasn't qualified for that job.

"I haven't seen you like this since…" Paddy shook his head. "Actually I don't think I've *ever* seen you like this."

"Like what?"

"Really aware of a woman. You haven't been…until now, until Tessa Howard."

"I'm not—"

"That really bothers you, doesn't it?" Paddy continued over Chad's protest. Even though the class continued to talk amongst themselves, Paddy lowered his voice to a raspy whisper. "You don't have to feel guilty, you know."

"Guilty?"

"That you've noticed a woman other than Luanne."

"Luanne's gone."

"Exactly," Paddy said as if he'd made his point.

But the watch commander had no idea what was in Chad's head—or his heart. And he didn't intend to share his regret and loss.

"We have a class to teach," Chad reminded his friend.

Actually to continue teaching. Before coming down to the parking garage, Chad had explained the pursuit decision-making model—in the warmth of the conference room. Tessa had missed all the discussion about what constituted low risk or high risk when officers were pursuing a speeding vehicle. Most of the CPA participants had been surprised to learn there were times the police chose not to pursue. When he'd explained about speeding through school zones and areas with numerous pedestrians, though, they had understood that the risk was too great. Which was the way he felt about getting involved with Tessa Howard.

"This session is all yours," Paddy agreed as he stepped back. He cleared his voice and raised it loud enough to reverberate off the cement walls of the parking garage. "Now Lieutenant Chad Michalski will be demonstrating traffic stop procedure."

Chad's last class. He could handle one more night with Tessa Howard. Maybe he could even find out what the hell she'd been doing in the park last week. Of course, he only cared because, as he'd told her, it was his job.

USUALLY TESSA would hate leaving a sales call for a class that she wouldn't be taking if not for the threat of losing her driver's license and therefore her job, but tonight she hadn't wanted to be late. She'd looked forward to seeing Brigitte and Erin and Bernie and her husband, Jimmy, and even Amy and the others. Heck, she'd looked forward all week to seeing every member of the citizens' police academy again.

She dragged in a breath to ease her irritation over her last appointment. The guy had been more interested in her than setting up an account. She clenched her fingers around the handle of her briefcase. He'd been married. Separated, he'd claimed. Even if he had been single, she wasn't interested.

Another man drew her gaze. Lieutenant Michalski, so tall

and lean in his black uniform, leaned against the side of his police car. But she wasn't interested in him, either.

"He could pull me over any time," Amy murmured.

"Remember you can't flirt your way out of a ticket with Lieutenant Michalski," Bernie Gillespie warned the girl. "It sure didn't work for Tessa."

Jimmy shook his head and murmured, "The guy must be made of stone."

A frigid wind whipped around the cement structure, chilling Tessa to the core, and she whispered, "At least his heart is…"

Sure, he'd offered to help her last week, but only because of his oath to protect and serve. If she'd actually confided in him, she might have gotten Kevin in trouble…even more trouble than Mr. Gillespie was in for his flirty comment.

"Jimmy!" Brigitte admonished the older man, then turned to his wife. "You're going to let him get away with that?"

"What?" Bernie shrugged. "I don't mind that he notices pretty girls. He has always been true to me."

"Because she's the prettiest girl of all," Jimmy dutifully proclaimed of his heavyset wife.

"*Now* whose eyesight's failing?" she chuckled.

"Every time I look at her, my heart skips a beat," Jimmy insisted as he pressed a meaty palm across his chest.

Bernie snorted. "We're going to have to have the doctor adjust that pacemaker again."

Tessa and Brigitte laughed.

"You're one of a kind, Jimmy," Brigitte said. "If they still made guys like you, I might actually dare to start dating again."

"I would, too," Tessa agreed. "If I had time…"

"Class!" Lieutenant Michalski said in a voice loud enough to echo in the parking garage. Then he focused on Tessa, as if she had been the one disrupting the group. "Who wants to volunteer for the first traffic stop? One citizen will ride in the car being pulled over." He gestured toward the unmarked police car. "And the other will ride in the patrol car."

Amy's hand shot up. "I want to ride with you!"

"Who wants to be pulled over?" he asked, glancing again at Tessa. The rest of the class turned to her, expectantly, as well.

She shook her head. "I have quite enough experience being pulled over, so I'll sit this one out and let someone else take a turn."

"I'll do it," Brigitte offered. She winked at Tessa. "I've never gotten a ticket."

If only Tessa could say the same. Yet the thought of not participating in the class, of not having met this group of fun, interesting people, had a sense of loss gripping her.

The siren rang out as it had when Chad had pulled her over last week, but it echoed off the cement partitions, and Tessa grimaced. A headache had been threatening all day with pressure behind her eyes and the back of her neck.

Since the cars only moved a few feet, with the simulated pullover, the demonstration ended quickly. Or maybe that was because Chad had had Amy in his vehicle. He stepped out of the police car, asking for the next volunteers.

"Us!" Bernie called out, pulling her much taller and heavier husband along behind her. "We want to go next."

Jimmy turned back to Tessa. "You're freezing out here. Why don't you get in the backseat while Bernie's operating the cruiser?"

"I'm fine," Tessa insisted.

But Jimmy reached out and caught her hand to tug her along with them. "Tessa's going to ride in the back to stay warm," he told Chad.

"I used to be a speed demon like Tessa," Bernie told the lieutenant, her eyes bright with pride and memories.

"She drag raced," Jimmy said.

Tessa laughed, more at the horrified expression on Chad's handsome face than at the image of the older woman behind the wheel of a dragster.

"No, I really did," Bernie insisted. "I loved to take chances. Live for the thrill."

"Still does," Jimmy grumbled. "That's how she talked me into this class."

"Really?" Tessa prodded with genuine interest because she had never known anyone married so long who still seemed truly happy.

"We keep the thrills in our relationship," Bernie said, with more pride. A successful marriage was a valid reason to be proud.

Chad shook his head. "Forget the thrills. I'd prefer safe and secure."

So would Tessa, but she snorted with derision. "Sounds boring," she said, because she figured it was the reaction he expected of her.

Chad held open the back door for her, putting his hand on the top of her head as she slid into the seat.

She turned toward him, her lips curving into a sassy smile. "You've been wanting to get me in the backseat of your car for a while," she teased.

Images of the two of them crawling—naked—all over each other in a backseat flashed through Chad's mind, and heat coursed through his body, chasing away the chill of the cold night.

"I haven't wanted to arrest you, Ms. Howard," he corrected her as he took the front seat with Mrs. Gillespie behind the wheel.

"You just want to ticket me?" she asked from behind the Plexiglas divider.

"I just want you to drive more carefully." That was all he wanted. All he *could* want.

Mrs. Gillespie threw the car into Drive and lurched forward, striking the rear bumper of the unmarked car. "Oh, damn," she said. "I forgot the siren." She clicked the button on the controller between the seats.

Chad, with his knees wedged against the dash now, whirled toward Tessa. "Are you all right?"

She rubbed her cheek from where her face had struck the divider. "I'm fine."

"Oh, I'm sorry, dear," Mrs. Gillespie said. As she turned toward Tessa, her foot came off the brake and they lurched forward, striking the other car again.

Chad reached over, shifted the car into Park and shut off the wailing siren. He stepped from the passenger's side and told the rest of the class, who were covering their ears with their hands, "That's how we *don't* pull someone over."

Mr. Gillespie vaulted out of the unmarked car and ran back to check on his wife. "Darling, are you all right?"

Chad shook his head, amazed that the man wasn't fuming mad, as he would have been. As he was...

He opened the back door and helped Tessa from the vehicle. He gently pulled away the hand she clutched to her cheek. Had she struck the metal frame as well as the Plexiglas? "It's red." The ridiculous urge to kiss it better prompted him to lean forward, but he caught himself. "You need some ice."

"That's why I had my hand against it," she said, tugging

her fingers free of his. Her skin was icy cold, goose bumps raised along her bare forearms.

"You're both okay?" he asked the Gillespies.

"That was exciting!" Mrs. proclaimed. "Like bumper cars."

Mr. chuckled, but he came over to Tessa, his eyes soft with concern. "You're all right?"

She nodded. "Fine. I think the lieutenant worked this all out with your wife." She lowered her voice to a conspiratorial whisper that was still loud enough for most of the class to hear. "He's been dying to knock some sense into me."

"If only it were that easy…" Chad mused aloud, drawing chortles from the rest of the class. "Okay, no serious damage done, so let's keep taking turns. Who wants to be in the unmarked car?"

Reverend Thomas, a youth minister, who didn't look much older than the teens he worked with, raised his hand. "I'll be the lawbreaker."

"Ohh, the minister's going to take a walk on the wild side," Leonard Romanski, a kid who was in college *because* of Reverend Thomas, teased. Maybe Leonard hadn't gone into criminal justice just for the groupies, although he seemed to have quite an interest in Amy.

Tessa started to walk away to join the rest of the class, but Chad caught her wrist. "You're going to pull him over," he said, walking her around the car to the driver's door which he held open for her.

"I really don't need to do this," she protested.

"You should check out things from this side of the traffic stop," he advised, shutting her inside the warm car. While she was probably too stubborn to learn much from the demonstration, at least he could keep her from freezing.

Once she was settled, he joined her inside the car. So little space separated the seats that his shoulder bumped against hers. He showed her the controls between the seats, pointing out the button for the siren and the one for the lights. The back of his hand brushed against her thigh, bare from her short skirt. She shivered.

His hand shaking slightly, he adjusted the heat. "You're still cold? You really need to dress warmer. Paddy noted in the academy outline which classes you'd need to dress warmer."

"I—I came straight from a sales call," she explained, her voice wavering either with cold or nerves.

He reached across her, making sure the vents were open on the driver's side. As he drew his hand away from the dash, he brushed her bare knee, and his face heated. Had to be because of the heat blowing full force on him.

"You could bring a change of clothes, you know," he pointed out.

"Uh, yeah, I guess I could."

"You haven't even glanced at the CPA binder," he realized. "You have no interest in this class at all."

She flashed her sassy smile again even though it looked a bit strained. Then she winked at him. "I wouldn't say that I have *no* interest in the class…"

Chad snorted. "You're not interested in me. You're trying to mess with my head." It was damn well working, too. Remembering his role as class instructor, he directed her, "Turn on the siren."

"I'd rather turn you on."

Even as his body tensed in reaction to her flirting, he laughed. "You're impossible."

She sighed. "That's what they all say."

"They're not wrong." Any attraction to her was impossible. Whether going too fast or too slow, the woman was always reckless. Definitely too high a risk factor for pursuit.

"COFFEE, PLEASE," Tessa requested, her teeth nearly clicking together as they chattered from the cold that had penetrated deep inside her body.

"Decaf?" Brigitte asked as she reached for a carafe.

"No, I need the real stuff," Tessa insisted.

"You'll be up all night." Brigitte arched a brow. "Ohh…"

"Oh, what?"

"Maybe you're *planning* on being up all night—with Lieutenant Michalski?"

Tessa choked on a laugh. "Not damn likely." No matter how much she flirted, he remained his usual stoic self. Maybe the man was made of stone. Not that she really wanted him interested in her.

She had flirted with him in the car during their simulated traffic stop only because he'd rattled her with his concern over her being hurt and with his touch as he'd brushed her thigh and knee. The competitive part of her had wanted to rattle him back. *More*.

Her trick had backfired because she'd realized the outrageous comment she had spoken was true. She *did* want to turn him on. Her hands trembled as she accepted the mug of coffee her friend passed her.

"Careful so you don't burn yourself," Brigitte advised, perhaps referring to more than the hot beverage. She had the uncanny perception of a bartender, which she would probably also deny as being a myth if Tessa pointed it out.

Yet Tessa wasn't about to admit her new friend was right and that she was in danger of getting burned. She carefully sipped from the mug.

Music emanated from the game area, and two voices in beautiful harmony rose above the conversations taking place in the Lighthouse.

"Karaoke?" Tessa asked.

Brigitte grimaced. "Yeah, it was my idea. Don't know what I was thinking."

"Cops doing karaoke?" Tessa laughed. "I think it's a great idea."

The bartender lifted her slender shoulders in a slight shrug. "I thought it might bring in more customers."

Tessa glanced around the bar, which was pretty much standing room only. "You want more?"

Brigitte grinned. "I want to make sure Gramps can retire comfortably. He's thinking about Key West."

"If it stays this packed—" Tessa gestured at the crowd "—he can probably retire in Palm Springs."

The beautiful bartender shook her head. "I think the machine has probably scared away more customers than it's attracted."

"Whoever's singing now is actually pretty good." Tessa smiled at the lyrics of the old Sonny and Cher tune. Swiveling the bar stool around to see who was singing, she laughed. "Bernie and Jimmy?"

Of course they would sing in perfect harmony. She had never met a more perfect couple; she hadn't thought anyone could have as long and solid a marriage as they shared. Maybe there was hope.

Chad joined her at the bar, squeezing in between her and the next occupied stool. "You warm yet?"

She lifted the coffee mug. "I'm getting there." Especially now, with him standing so close that his hard thigh rubbed against her hip.

"That's good."

"And those two help," she said, pointing toward the karaoke couple. "What they have…it just kinda warms you up."

He glanced toward the makeshift stage near the pool tables and dartboards, then back to Tessa. A muscle twitched in his cheek as if he clenched his jaw. "Yeah…"

After another sip of the hot brew, she asked, "You ever been married?"

He tensed. "A long time ago."

"One of those high school sweetheart things that burned out?"

His green eyes darkened with pain. "College sweethearts."

He still hurt over the broken relationship? "How long ago did you divorce?" she asked.

He shrugged without answering, then asked, "Did you have a college sweetheart?"

She sighed, unable to call any of the men she'd dated a *sweetheart*. "I didn't go away to college. I took night classes in sales and marketing at the local community college."

"Since you're used to taking night classes, why do you have such a problem with this one?" he asked, his mouth lifting in a slight grin.

"I signed up for those classes *voluntarily*."

"So you don't like being told what to do," he said with a nod of his dark head. "That's why you didn't wear the warm clothes that were recommended for tonight's class?"

"No, I didn't read the binder," she confirmed his earlier suspicion. "But I came right from an appointment, so I didn't have time to change or even grab a change of clothes anyway."

"If you had time," he asked, leaning in so that his face nearly touched hers, "would you change?"

Somehow she suspected they weren't talking about just her clothes anymore. "The problem is," she said, "that I never have time."

Not for herself, and certainly not for a man, no matter how attractive she found him. Why the hell did she have to find Lieutenant Chad Michalski so attractive?

"Is that the reason you take late-night drives through the park?" he asked. "No time during the day?"

"Yeah, something like that."

"Are you ever going to tell me what was going on with you that night?"

She shook her head. "No point. I have it all under control." Too bad she was lying through her teeth. Kevin was still doing a great impersonation of an invisible man; he took off so much she hardly ever saw him.

"You're independent," he murmured.

"That's probably the one thing you actually have right about me, Lieutenant," she said.

"So what do I have wrong?" he asked.

The clamor of applause saved her from replying.

"Encore, encore!" the patrons shouted as the Gillespies finished their second duet.

"No, someone else has to take a turn," Bernie insisted. "It's quite a thrill. Lieutenant O'Donnell?"

The auburn-haired lawman, sitting with his CPA class at the long table, shook his head. "No. No, you don't want to hear me sing."

"I'll sing," Amy said as she nearly skipped to the karaoke machine.

Even with caffeine rushing through her veins, Tessa didn't have a tenth of the college girl's energy. She had never been that young and carefree. And she sure couldn't sing like that. Amy's voice was soft and pure as she sang of falling in love. The girl was actually very good.

Bernie stepped into Jimmy's arms, and they began to

dance. Other members of the CPA pushed the long table against the wall, giving the couple more space. Bernie lifted her hand from Jimmy's shoulder, and motioned for others to join her.

"Do you sing?" Tessa asked Chad.

Chad shook his head. "Nope, I don't sing. You?"

She shuddered. "No."

"I dance. Do you dance?"

"Sure, I dance." Although she couldn't remember the last time.

"So?" He held out his hand.

What the hell was he thinking? Asking Tessa Howard to dance was a mistake, an impulse. He hadn't acted on impulses since he'd been a reckless kid what seemed like a hundred years ago.

Tessa gazed up at him, her blue eyes wide with shock. Then, to his surprise, she placed her hand in his. "Sure, I'll dance."

Fingers entwined, they walked across the bar and joined the others on the makeshift dance floor. The pimply-faced kid, Leonard Ramanski danced with Marla Halliday, the vice cop's mother, who had entered the academy to find out how safe her son was on the job. She probably wouldn't like what she learned.

And Chad didn't like what he learned as he opened his arms and Tessa Howard stepped into them, her body brushing against his as they moved to the music. *He wanted her.* Despite knowing that she would be no good for him, he wanted her.

"Are—are you warmer now?" he asked, as he slid his hand over her back.

"What?" She tipped up her chin and stared into his face.

"You were so cold in the parking garage. Are you warmer now?"

"Is that why you asked me to dance?" She stopped moving. "To warm me up?"

"I wish to hell I knew…why…" She was so damn beautiful, but it was more than her beauty that drew him. It was her spirit and humor—she was so alive that she made him feel alive. And he hadn't been really alive since Luanne died.

"It worked," she murmured. "I'm warmed up…"

In fact her face was flushed, her eyes bright. Then her lips parted.

And he leaned forward just far enough for his mouth to brush across hers.

Chapter Seven

Her lips tingling from the all-too-brief contact with his, Tessa opened her eyes—and found herself standing alone on the makeshift dance floor among the other couples. She was no longer a couple, but then she had never really been. *Ever*.

Face warm with embarrassment, she smiled as she moved off the floor and headed toward the bar. She glanced around but couldn't see Chad anywhere. He must have left in a hurry.

"Who's speeding now?" she murmured. The man hadn't been able to move fast enough to get away from her. "I should've given him a ticket."

"What ticket?" Brigitte asked as Tessa settled onto her stool at the bar. "Tonight's class was just a demonstration. No one got any tickets."

She shook her head. "No, that's not what I was talking about."

"Want more coffee?" Brigitte asked, lifting the carafe.

Tessa placed her hand over the top of her mug. "No thanks. I really need to go home."

"Stay," Lieutenant O'Donnell requested as he slid onto the empty bar stool next to her. "Join me for a cup of coffee."

"Regular or decaf?" Brigitte asked.

"I need the unleaded," the lieutenant said, "or I won't sleep at all tonight."

"And that would be different *how?*" Brigitte teased as she passed him a mug before moving on to serve other customers.

"You don't sleep?" Tessa asked, turning toward the watch commander. "Lieutenant Michalski isn't the only one with demons, then."

"We all have demons, Ms. Howard," O'Donnell philosophized, "I suspect even you."

She flashed her patented flirty smile. "You tell me yours, I'll tell you mine."

He grinned as if flattered by her flirting, but shook his head. "You don't want to know mine, Ms. Howard. You want to know *his.*"

She couldn't hang on to the smile. "His? I don't know who you're talking about."

"You know."

"I don't want to know," she said, sliding off the stool. "I have to go home."

The lieutenant caught her arm, keeping her from leaving. "His wife died four years ago."

Tessa's breath caught in her lungs. "His college sweetheart?"

"Yes."

His wife hadn't divorced Chad because she'd learned he wasn't perfect. "She died…"

"She died in a *traffic* accident."

"Oh."

"She was speeding," O'Donnell continued, his hand tightening on her arm. "Going too fast to stop for the light that had just turned red."

"Oh."

"And she was pregnant."

"Oh, my God." Pain clutched her, pain for what Chad had gone through and for what he'd lost.

How had he managed to get out of bed every morning for the past four years? How did he go to a job that surely must remind him of what he'd lost and how?

His reaction to the footage of the traffic accident suddenly made sense—as did his overreaction to her speeding. He wanted to save other people from suffering the same loss he had.

The watch commander, who was obviously a very close friend to Chad, said, "The doctors took the baby by cesarean, but he was too premature. He lasted through a few surgeries to repair damage from the accident. He survived a couple of weeks—then Chad had to decide whether to put him through more procedures or let him go."

Tears stung her eyes over the impossible decision Chad had had to make. With certainty she said, "He let him go." He would not have allowed anyone, let alone someone he loved, to suffer.

Lieutenant O'Donnell sighed. "Not yet. Not really. I don't think he's let either of them go yet."

Pain clutched Tessa again—for what *she* had lost before she'd even had it—a chance with a guy who would have stuck around. But he was already doing that—he was sticking with his dead wife and child—and his feelings for them.

Her released a shaky sigh. "Thank you for telling me."

"I should have told you last week," the lieutenant said with self-recrimination, "when you asked about Chad."

"I understand," she assured him. "You were being a good friend by protecting his privacy." She doubted many people knew Chad's business except those very close to him. Now she knew that she would *never* be one of those people.

"I think I'm being a better friend now," O'Donnell said, "by letting you know what demons he has."

"A good friend to Chad or me?" she asked. "Because now you've warned me away."

"That wasn't my intention," Paddy insisted. "I want you to understand him."

She nodded. "I do. I understand why he doesn't like me and why he will never care about any woman like he did his wife." His college sweetheart, the love of his life. No woman could really compete with his memories of her, so Tessa refused to even try.

She hadn't had time for the men who had actually been interested in her.

"I have to go home," she said again.

"This was Chad's last class," the watch commander said, "you're not going to see him for a while."

Probably not ever again. Remembering how he'd run off after that mere brush of their lips, Tessa doubted that Chad would seek her out. He probably felt guilty, as if he'd betrayed his wife. Despite the many offers, Tessa intended to be no man's mistress.

HER HAND TREMBLED as Tessa fumbled inside her briefcase for her keys, but she could barely see the contents in the dim light of the parking lot. She should have found them while she was still inside, but she couldn't wait to get away from the watch commander and from what he'd told her. Chad's demons chased her now.

Both figuratively and maybe literally. A hulking shadow separated from the others around the back of the Lighthouse, and shoes scuffed against the asphalt as someone crossed the parking lot toward her. She uttered a squeak of surprise and dropped her briefcase.

"You're acting recklessly again," Chad censored her. "You're making yourself a prime target for an attack. Distracted, ill-prepared."

Which was all *his* fault. "So are you going to attack me?"

"I'm sorry," he said.

"About kissing me?"

He was sorry he'd stopped, but he never should have given in to temptation. "The dance—everything—was a mistake."

"Agreed."

Pride stinging from her fast agreement and with the twinge of jealousy he had felt when he'd caught the smile she'd flashed his friend, he said, "I saw you drinking with Paddy."

"Want to administer a Breathalyzer? See if I'm fit to drive?" she challenged him.

"Even though you were drinking coffee, I *know* you're not fit to drive."

"Maybe you're not fit to judge that."

"What do you mean?" But he knew. They'd been so deep in conversation that they hadn't even noticed him. "He told you, didn't he? Paddy told you?"

"About your wife?" She nodded. "Yes, he told me." Her voice soft with sympathy, she added, "I'm very sorry for your loss."

Because they'd always made him uncomfortable, he ignored her condolences and remarked, "You remind me of her."

"I look like her?"

"Not at all." Luanne had had dark hair and brown eyes, which had always brimmed with laughter. She'd laughed at him every time he'd warned her to slow down. "You act like her." And she made him feel what Luanne had—she made him *feel,* something he hadn't done in years.

"Just because I speed? I think the majority of drivers speed," she insisted, "but those aren't statistics you're likely to share with the class."

"I'm done with the class," he said, expelling a breath of relief. "Tonight ended my participation in the program."

"So Lieutenant O'Donnell said."

"It's not just the speeding you have in common with Luanne."

"Luanne? That's a pretty name."

"She was a pretty girl," he said, remembering the first time he'd met her, dancing on a table at a frat party, "and vivacious." He smiled, remembering her boundless energy. "And carefree. So carefree that she was actually *careless*."

"Just because she drove a little over the limit?" Tessa asked, defending a woman she'd never met. Yet just because she'd never met Luanne didn't mean she didn't know her. As Chad had pointed out, the two women were a lot alike.

"It was more than that. Luanne never drove just a *little* over the limit." In college, they'd been like Bernie and Jimmy— eager for thrills—but when Chad had started working for the department, he'd changed. He'd tried to get Luanne to change, too.

"It was an *accident*, Chad," she said softly, as she slid her fingers over his forearm. "They call them that for a reason. She didn't do it on purpose."

"No, she didn't do it on purpose," he agreed. "But she did a lot of other crazy things on purpose. She bungee jumped. She went sky diving, white-water rafting."

Tessa smiled. "She sounds like fun."

"She was." She'd even talked him into doing most of those crazy things with her.

"You still miss her."

"Every day."

"But you also resent her."

He resented that she'd taken away all the joy she'd brought to his life. "I just wanted her to slow down a little." Especially when she got pregnant. "But she wanted to experience every thrill before she died."

Tessa mused, "Almost as if she knew she didn't have much time…"

"She would have had more—" *They* would have had more. "—if she had been more careful. But she thought she was invincible." He swallowed hard. "She wasn't."

"And neither am I," Tessa agreed. "That's all Luanne and I really have in common. All I guess anyone has in common. Because no one's invincible."

"If you know that, why are *you* so careless?" Chad asked as he bent down to pick up her briefcase from the asphalt. Some of the contents had spilled out, including her keys, the metal of which glinted in the dim glow of the street lamps. "You're lucky it was me standing out here, waiting for you."

He'd seen too much on the job, knew what could happen so quickly to someone who'd dropped her guard, who'd become distracted…

"Why?" she asked, her voice quiet and her eyes wide as she stared up at him. "Why were you waiting for me? Just to apologize?"

"No," he admitted to her—and to himself.

He had dated a few women after Luanne died—casually. Dinner, movies, a couple of times even more. He was a widower not a monk. But those times, he hadn't felt as much as he had from just brushing his lips over Tessa's soft, sexy mouth. For that reason, he should have run. He had confirmation now that the risk was too high for pursuit.

"Then why did you wait for me?" she persisted.

He grabbed up her keys and pressed them into her palm. "To finish what I started."

For a moment—just a moment—Tessa's heart stopped beating, then resumed at a crazy pace. "What are you talking about?"

His palms cupped her face, which he tipped up to his. "Our dance."

"But there's no music."

"Yes, there is."

"I can't hear it."

"Close your eyes and listen."

Tessa obeyed, but she heard nothing…until his lips touched her. Then as his mouth moved hungrily over hers, she caught the words of a love song…playing on the wind. Yet she knew that song would never be theirs. Even knowing that his heart belonged to someone else, though, she kissed him back. She lifted her hands to his wide shoulders and pulled him closer.

His tongue slid across her bottom lip and then into her mouth, tangling with hers. Breath burned in her lungs, but she didn't care. She didn't need to breathe with his mouth on hers. She needed only him.

He pulled back and leaned his forehead against hers. "God, Tessa, I wish…"

"That I was Luanne?" she asked, her heart hurting over the regret on his handsome face. Was that why he had kissed her? To recapture what he'd lost?

He shook his head. "Of course not…"

"I'm sorry, Lieutenant, but no matter how much I might remind you of her, I'm not your dead wife." She tightened her hand around her keys until the metal dug deep into her palm.

"I know."

Was that why he'd stopped kissing her? Because she

wasn't the woman he really wanted? She didn't care to find out. She had enough baggage of her own; she couldn't carry anyone else's.

"Goodbye, Chad."

THE INCESSANT RINGING of his doorbell drew Chad from his bed. He stumbled across the living room toward the front door of his condo. Glimpsing the distinctive black Lakewood PD uniform through the stained glass sidelight, he figured Paddy had given up calling to apologize for spilling Chad's secrets to Tessa and intended to say sorry in person.

Before opening the door to his friend, Chad turned back toward his coffee table, checking to make sure he had tucked away all his pictures inside the leather box nearly covering the surface of the dark wood. He always intended to put the box in storage yet could never quite bring himself to part with it.

He had pored over his wedding album all night, worried that he might have begun to forget how Luanne looked on that day. How her dark eyes had shone with happiness and love.

Had he imagined it all or had they really been that happy? Looking at those pictures, he'd remembered his own euphoria. A man didn't get a chance at happiness that complete more than once.

He opened the door, fully intending to blast his friend for his interference no matter how well intentioned it had probably been. But Paddy wasn't the Lakewood officer who had come for a visit. "Chief?"

The guy was so tall he nearly had to duck to clear the doorway as he stepped inside the condo. "Nice place, Lieutenant," he said even though he barely glanced around.

"What brings you by?" Chad asked as he noted the early hour.

"I've made a decision. I am going to sell the house," Archer shared. "So I wanted to get the name of the Realtor you used."

Chad's brow furrowed. "That was four years ago."

"He or she isn't selling real estate anymore?"

"Well, he actually didn't sell my house," Chad admitted. "With the market what it was then, it was smarter to rent the house." Because then he hadn't had to completely let go. He realized now that that was why he'd kept it.

"So you're still renting it out?"

When he could find qualified renters…

Chad nodded. "Yeah, the market hasn't improved yet."

"And when it does?" Archer asked, "Will you sell it then?"

"Of course."

The chief narrowed his eyes, asking a question with just that pointed look.

"I will," Chad assured him, even though he wasn't convinced himself. Letting go of the house she'd joyfully decorated, letting go of the pictures that had captured their happiness—letting go of *Luanne* wasn't something he was ready to do just yet. "What about you? What's made you decide to sell your house?"

Or who?

The chief shrugged. "It's time."

"It's only been a year," Chad reminded him although he doubted the other man needed a reminder. Chad could mark to the day how long Luanne had been gone. The chief had had his wife longer—wouldn't he miss her more instead of less?

"It's time," Frank Archer repeated, staring hard at his lieutenant.

"You talked to Paddy," Chad guessed, irritation scraping across his nerves. "He sent you here?"

"No. I really came for the Realtor's name. And to check out this place." The chief looked around again, taking in the small galley kitchen and living area. "I thought if I liked it, I might look into buying a condo in this complex."

"And now?"

"I realized what this is."

"What is it?" Chad wondered, glancing around at his spartan living room.

"Limbo."

"What? I don't understand," he claimed, even though he was damn sure the chief had him all figured out. It probably took one to know one.

"You're caught between your past and the present, Chad," Frank Archer pointed out. "Until you let the past go, you're never going to move forward—you're never going to have a future."

He had buried his future four years ago. Tessa Howard's voice echoed in his head—calling him a hypocrite. He closed his eyes and saw her beautiful face, her blue eyes staring up at him…as if she cared, as if she could care…if he let her.

He couldn't let her; she deserved more.

Chapter Eight

Tessa dug through her briefcase in search of her keys. Memories of the last time she had lost them—in the parking lot of the Lighthouse—flitted through her mind. She should have been more vigilant, more careful. She never should have made out with a man still in love with his dead wife.

Now she was home, in the kitchenette of her walkout basement apartment. She didn't have to be careful at home, alone—or as relatively alone as she was ever going to get with her family.

Metal clinked against metal, and she turned to the patio doors, where her brother Kevin twirled her key chain around his finger. "Looking for these?"

"Yes," she said. "Hand them over right now, and I'll let you live despite your snooping through my stuff."

"I wasn't snooping," Kevin objected. "It's not like I was looking for your diary or anything."

"Which would have been a waste of your time," she said, "since I don't have one."

"No wonder." He snorted. "What the hell would you write in a diary? You never do anything but work and watch the kids."

"Don't swear," she admonished him, "and you should be watching the littler kids."

Color flushed his fair skin. "I'm busy."

Tessa groaned. "That's what scares me."

"What?"

"Your being busy. Just what are you busy doing, little brother?" she asked as she walked up in front of him. Her "little" brother towered over her by half a foot.

"Nothing."

She cringed at his evasiveness. "I lay awake nights worrying about what you consider 'nothing.'"

"Don't worry about me. I'm not *your* kid," he said. "None of us are."

She narrowed her eyes to study him. He was blond like her, but his hair was spiked. He wore a wrinkly T-shirt and ragged jeans that sagged low on his skinny hips.

"What do you mean by that?" she asked, trying to gauge his strange mood.

"Nothing…"

She closed her eyes. "That word again."

"I'll change it to *something*."

"Something?" She sighed. "You *want* something."

"I need to get in my hours." He spun the key ring again. "I can't get my license until I get in more practice driving."

"Kevin…" She shook her head. Despite it being Saturday, she was still busy. "I can't right now. I have some errands to run. I have to go."

"Let me drive you for your errands," he persisted. "I'll be your chauffeur."

"I like to drive myself."

Kevin snorted again. "Yeah, look where that got you—almost thrown in jail."

And she had thought Audrey the overly dramatic one. "I'm not in jail."

"You have to take that class."

"I like that…" She trailed off, stunned by her involuntary admission. "I like that class."

"Good," Kevin said, "you should do something you like for once."

"This class isn't the only thing I do that I like," Tessa insisted. "I like my job."

"You just like working there because you need the money," Kevin said. "For us. You have to watch us…since Mom's never around."

"She's around when she's not working," Tessa defended their mother. "She may be around more. I talked to a friend about getting her a job as a day-shift bartender."

"That would be good," he said, then met her gaze. "For all of us."

"Yes." Touched that he seemed so concerned about her, Tessa reached out and passed her hand over his spiky hair the way she did with her smaller brothers.

The lanky teenager ducked away from her. "Hey, don't mess with the 'do, Tess!"

She lifted both arms and ran her hands through his hair, then grimaced and wiped her gel-covered fingers on his shirt. "You know what else would be better for everyone?" she teased. "If you never got your license."

He ignored her comment and her sticky handprints and goaded her, "Come on, Tess, I'll race you to the Suburban." He pulled open the patio door and headed up the stairs to the driveway.

"Kevin!" she yelled as she grabbed her briefcase and headed out after him. "Come back here!" The SUV engine started, and she ran faster. "Kevin!"

Before he could pull out of the driveway, she jerked open

the passenger's door and jumped inside. "Okay, I'll let you drive, but you have to take it slowly and carefully."

"What's this? Do as I say, not as I do?" he quipped with a cocky grin.

"Smartass."

"Don't swear."

"Don't drive so fast!" she warned him as he pressed on the accelerator.

"Hey, who's got more tickets?"

"You better not have *any,*" she threatened him.

"You're the one who gets all the tickets, Tess," he said, without really answering her question. "You're the lousy driver."

"If I'm so lousy," she challenged him, "how come you want to drive with me?"

"It's safer for me to drive you than have you drive me." He grinned. "I think you really do need a chauffeur."

"Smartass—"

This time the wail of a siren cut her off. She turned her head and glimpsed red and blue lights flashing through the rear window.

"What do I do?" Kevin asked, his voice shaking with panic.

"Pull over," she advised, "slowly and carefully."

"B-but there're never any cops on our street," Kevin protested as he steered the SUV to the curb and shifted it into Park.

She wouldn't put it past Chad to have set up a speed trap on her street to catch her exceeding the limit again. She closed her eyes, not wanting to see him if he was the officer who'd stopped them.

"Tess!" Kevin whispered urgently. "What do I do?"

"Roll down the window," she directed.

"License, please," a masculine voice requested.

Tessa sighed with relief and opened her eyes. It wasn't

Chad. She glanced to the window and the young officer leaning close to it.

"I just have a permit," Kevin said as he pulled it from his pocket.

"Then, Miss, I'll need to see your license and registration and your certificate of insurance."

Tessa pulled them from her briefcase and passed them to Kevin who, his hand shaking as badly as his voice, passed them to the officer. The guy glanced at the license and then leaned closer to the window, peering at Tessa. "You're the lieutenant's lady."

"What?"

"You're Lieutenant Michalski's girl," the officer insisted with a wide grin.

"No—no, I'm not." Had someone seen them in the parking lot the other night?

Kevin reached across the console and pinched her arm. "Yes, yes, she is."

The officer nodded. "I thought that was you—from the elevator."

The elevator. She fisted her hands to prevent herself from burying her warm face in her palms. "Oh…"

His grin widened. "Although you were exceeding the speed limit by seven miles, I'll let you off with a warning this time."

"The lieutenant wouldn't." Pain shot up her arm as Kevin pinched her again, harder.

The young officer laughed as if she was joking. Didn't he know Chad? Apparently not very well as he waved at her and walked back to his car.

"What are you trying to do?" Kevin asked. "Oh, yeah, you want me to get a ticket so that I *never* get my license."

"This isn't about you," she said through gritted teeth. She

wasn't Chad's girlfriend. How could she continue the class with everyone thinking that she was, or that she was like the starstruck Amy and wanted to be?

"That's good," Kevin said as he studied her face. "You need something that isn't about me or the rest of the kids."

"You said that earlier about the class," she remembered, "What's gotten into you? Have you been watching Dr. Phil with these invisible friends of yours?"

He pinched her again before putting the SUV back in Drive and pulling away from the curb. "The class is good for you, but it's even better that you're dating," he said. "With the lousy way you drive, you're really smart to date a cop, too."

"I'm not dating him," she insisted.

"Maybe you should," he suggested. "Until this class, I don't remember the last time you went out for anything besides work. You never date."

"I don't have time," she said, wondering if it was really true or just an excuse she used to keep from getting hurt the way her mother always did. Certainly she wasn't that much of a coward?

"I'm always busy with you guys," she insisted. Nana had always put her family first, so Tessa intended to do the same.

"Talk Mom into letting me get my license and then I can drive everyone around and you won't need to worry about us," Kevin urged her. "You can have your own life *finally,* Tess."

"I have my own life."

"All you have right now is that class."

With Chad so obviously still in love with his dead wife, the class and the new friends she was making were likely all she'd have. That was fine with her. Great, really; she didn't want anything more. She had her family, her career, her friends now— she didn't *need* a man. She was *not* her mother's daughter.

DESPITE THE WATCH COMMANDER telling her the week before had been the last of Chad's class participation, she glanced toward the front of the room, scanning the officers' table for him. But she caught no glimpse of dark hair, no glint of green eyes. He was gone.

Gone from the class and gone from her life.

While they spent the first half of the night listening to the director of the 911 call center and the second half listening to actual 911 calls in the command center itself, Tessa felt none of the excitement her fellow classmates did. For her, without Chad, the spark of interest she'd had in the CPA had been snuffed out.

She barely paid attention as they wrapped up the evening back in the third-floor meeting room.

"Before we conclude for the night," Lieutenant O'Donnell said from the officers' table, which he shared with only Kent Terlecki now, "I'll hand out the ride-along assignments."

At the watch commander's insistence, Tessa had finally turned in her release form. She didn't remember which had been more daunting, signing away her right to sue if she were hurt on the ride-along or choosing a couple of dates she'd be available. Ultimately she'd put off the inevitable, and had chosen dates as close to the end of the program as she'd been able.

Tessa pulled out her PDA. While she hadn't wanted to participate in the program and especially not in the ride-along, she had actually changed her mind. She wanted to know more than the videos had shown about the day in a life of an officer, but not just any officer. She wanted to know what a day of Chad's life was like. Somehow she suspected all his days were only about work now.

"First I'll read out the citizen's name," O'Donnell said,

"then the date and then the officer to which the citizen has been assigned."

Amy leaned close and whispered, "No offense, but I hope I get Lieutenant Michalski."

"No offense taken," Tessa assured her. Instead of jealousy over the girl's blatant interest in Chad, pity filled her. Maybe she should warn the girl that no living woman was going to get Lieutenant Michalski's interest.

When O'Donnell read off Amy's name, he followed it with a female officer's name. Tessa bit her lip to keep from laughing at the girl's deflated expression. Erin, sitting on the other side of her, wasn't as successful at holding in a soft chuckle of amusement.

"Erin Powell," the watch commander announced, causing the reporter to tense. "Your participation in this academy has compelled me to change one of my rules."

Erin sucked in a breath and murmured to Tessa. "He's not going to let me go out on a ride-along."

While Tessa liked the young reporter, she could understand why—the woman hadn't actually made any friends in the department or necessarily with the rest of the class. Instead of meeting Lieutenant O'Donnell's gaze, though, Erin stared straight at the man sitting at the table next to him—the golden-haired public information officer.

When O'Donnell read off a date, Erin turned back to him. "The exception to my rule," he continued, "is that *I'll* be taking you out myself."

"I can attest," Kent Terlecki spoke up, "that since his promotion, it takes a lot to get Paddy out from behind his desk." He winked at Erin, almost as if flirting with her.

The reporter, her face flushed with color, turned to Tessa. "Nothing gets *him* out from behind his desk."

While the rest of the class clamored for ride-alongs with the CPA leader, Erin Powell was disappointed. Obviously she would have rather ridden with another man.

"Tessa Howard."

She glanced up and smiled at Lieutenant O'Donnell, then punched in the date he read off. While she had a couple of appointments already lined up for that evening, she'd move them to another time.

"You'll be riding along with Lieutenant Michalski, our EVO expert."

Apparently the lieutenant wasn't out of her life just yet. Somehow she suspected he wouldn't be any happier about that than she was.

CHAD REACHED for the bowl of pretzels and peanuts; he'd eaten his burger and fries a while ago. Now he sipped a glass of ginger ale and waited. *I should be at home.*

But the condo he'd bought after he'd lost his family wasn't a home. He wasn't quite ready to call it what the chief had, though. It wasn't limbo, it was just a place to sleep—when he could sleep. Thoughts of Tessa and kissing her kept him awake.

Because the condo was so quiet, he'd also come to the bar for noise, but he'd gotten more than he'd bargained for. The karaoke machine had been turned on again, and what was coming out of it could hardly be considered singing. A feminine voice shouted out the lyrics of "I Fought the Law."

A rookie walked up to the bar, ordered a beer, then caught sight of Chad and grinned. "Your lady—she's not much of a singer," he said, pointing toward the game area. "But she sure is hot."

"My lady?" He cocked his head, listening to the off-key voice.

"You don't recognize her?" Paddy asked, as he joined them, sliding onto the empty stool next to him.

Chad stood up, but for all the people gathered around, clapping, he couldn't catch a glimpse of the woman singing. "Tessa? That's Tessa singing?"

"Yeah, your girl is the hottest thing in the bar," the rookie said with an appreciative, lusty sigh.

Chad turned to the younger man with a glare. "She's not my girl."

"But—but…"

Then Paddy laughed. "That denial came a little late, Chad."

The rookie laughed, too. "She said the same thing when I pulled her over the other day."

"She said *what?*"

"That she wasn't your lady."

Of course she wouldn't think that she was. She would know that the kiss meant nothing…

"Wait a minute," he said, grabbing the kid's arm before he could walk away. "You pulled her over? *You pulled her over?*"

The rookie nodded. "Yeah, but I'm sorry. I—I didn't know who she was—"

His grip tightened on the other guy's arm. "What did you pull her over for?"

"Speeding," the young officer answered matter-of-factly, probably because everyone knew her driving record.

"Damn it!" She was never going to slow down—just as he'd feared. Just like Luanne. He released the kid and curled his fingers into a fist.

"She wasn't the one actually speeding. She was the passenger," the officer explained. "When I saw it was her, I let them go with a warning."

Them? Who the hell had she been with? He'd be damned if he'd ask a rookie more about the woman everyone considered his lady, though.

He settled back onto his stool. "I wouldn't have let her go…"

"That's what she said," the young officer replied as he walked away from the bar.

"Well, that was a lie," Paddy said as he reached for the bowl of peanuts and pretzels.

"What?" Chad asked, sparing his *friend* a glare. "You know Tessa Howard is *not* my lady."

"That's not what I was talking about." Paddy tossed a peanut into his mouth. "You did let her go."

"She wouldn't be in the class if I let her go," he pointed out.

"I'm not talking about a traffic stop, Chad, and you know it," the watch commander insisted. "She's interested in you, but you let her go."

He shook his head. "She's not interested in me."

"Do you know why I told her about Luanne?"

"No. But I've been meaning to talk to you about that." He just hadn't been ready yet, so he'd been avoiding Paddy as much as possible during the past week.

"I told her," Paddy explained, "because she asked me."

"So," Chad said, not quite ready to forgive his friend for interfering, "would you have told Kent's reporter if she asked?"

"Erin Powell wouldn't have asked about *you*," the watch commander pointed out. "*Tessa* did. Because she's interested in you."

Chad sighed. "She hates me because I forced her into this class."

"Yeah, she looks like she's having a horrible time." Paddy gestured toward the long table where the CPA had gathered.

While she hadn't sat down yet, Tessa crouched among the others with one arm around Jimmy and the other Bernie. Her hair poured like gold down her back. She'd ditched her jacket again so that she wore just a lacy tank top in an off-white color nearly the same hue as her creamy skin. Her skirt was red and short.

His hand shaking slightly, he reached for his ginger ale and downed it in a thirsty gulp. His mouth was still dry. The rookie was right—she was the hottest woman in the bar.

"She's going to have a great time on her ride-along, too," Paddy said.

"I hope you don't still have some crazy idea that she needs to ride-along with me," Chad said. Suddenly his body tensed with dread—or maybe anticipation—because he knew his friend was all about crazy ideas lately. Tessa Howard interested in *him? Yeah, right...*

On the other hand, she had kissed him back.

"You're the only officer I could assign her to," Paddy insisted.

"C'mon..."

"*You're* the reason she's in the program," Paddy reminded him. "And *you're* the one who can teach her the most about safe driving."

Apparently she hadn't learned anything about that yet since she had recently been riding in a speeding car.

So whom had she been riding with when the rookie pulled her over? Jealousy formed a hard knot in his stomach as he considered the possible choice.

HER FACE warm with embarrassment, Tessa tightened her hold around Jimmy's and Bernie's necks. "I can't believe I let you two talk me into that."

"It was a thrill, wasn't it?" Bernie asked with a chuckle.

Tessa wished it had been as big a thrill as Chad's kiss, then maybe she could get it—and him—out of her mind. "I'm not sure what I'd call that."

"You got a standing ovation," Bernie persisted.

"That wasn't for her singing," Jimmy murmured.

"Oh, Jimmy, you sweetie," Tessa said as she bussed a kiss on the bald spot atop his head. "You better be careful, Bernie, or I'm going to try to steal him from you."

Bernie chuckled again. "You wouldn't be the first woman to try."

"And fail," Jimmy reminded her. "I'm not going anywhere. I'm a one-woman man." He grabbed his wife's hand and squeezed. "This woman's."

Tessa smiled at the obvious love between the older couple and wished she would one day find such a love for herself. She knew it wouldn't be with Chad. Like Jimmy, he was a one-woman man, too. Luanne's. So Tessa would forget about his kiss—and she'd forget all about him. Once their ride-along was over—unless she could talk Lieutenant O'Donnell into switching her to another officer.

She caught sight of the watch commander at the bar. "Excuse me," she told the Gillespies. "All that singing worked up a thirst."

"I don't think that's why you're heading to the bar, dear," Bernie said, wriggling her eyebrows up and down.

Tessa glanced to the bar again and noted the man sitting next to O'Donnell. Even though it was the first time she'd seen him out of uniform, she recognized the broad shoulders in the gray T-shirt. Faded jeans hugged his butt and long legs. Now she really needed a drink.

"Why don't you ask him to dance again, and Jimmy and I will sing a romantic ballad for you," Bernie suggested.

Tessa shook her head. "No, thanks. I have no intention of dancing with the lieutenant a second time." She had no intention of riding with him, either.

Before she could get through the crowd to the bar, O'Donnell disappeared into the sea of shoulder-to-shoulder bodies. She probably should have tried to find him, but instead she continued forward—to Chad.

He turned to look at her, almost as if he'd sensed her approach. A policeman's instincts or something more? No, she had already accepted that they could have nothing more.

"Was it your idea?" she asked.

"What? Your singing? No sane person would have wanted that to happen," he quipped.

Unamused, she glared at him. "I'm not talking about my singing."

She really wished no one would bring it up again, but she knew not to hold her breath. She had siblings, after all, who had made it their mission to never let her live down any humiliation.

"I wouldn't talk about your singing, either," Chad teased, his mouth lifting in a slight grin.

Tessa's pulse quickened. Why did he have to be so damn handsome? She wouldn't let his good looks distract her; she wouldn't moon over him like Amy.

"I was talking about the ride-along," she explained. "Was it your idea for me to ride with you?"

The smile slid from his face. "No. I told Paddy it's a bad move, but I couldn't change his mind."

When thinking he had orchestrated the assignment, she'd been irritated. Knowing now that he was actually more opposed to it than she was actually hurt. She released a shaky sigh.

"Yeah, I'm frustrated, too," he said. "There's no talking to Paddy once he's made up his mind."

What about Chad? He'd obviously made up his mind about her. She doubted he'd change it. She turned to walk away, but a strong hand closed around her bare arm, holding her in place at his side.

Chad followed her gaze to his fingers against her bare skin. He shouldn't have stopped her, but he hadn't wanted her to leave. "I—I hear you're still speeding."

Her blue eyes widened. "Remember, you pulled me over last for going too slow."

She had never shared with him what had sent her out that night, driving through the park.

"That wasn't the last time you've been pulled over," he said. "One of the rookies…"

"Oh, I should have known he'd tell you."

"Because he thinks you're my lady."

She snorted. "We both know you don't consider me a *lady*. You consider me a pain in the ass."

"I don't know what I consider you, Tessa Howard." He just wished he didn't consider her at all. "Too stubborn to learn from your mistakes, apparently."

"I was not the one speeding," she said.

His voice rough, he asked the question that had been driving him crazy since talking to the rookie. "Then who were you riding with?"

She arched a blond brow. "Jealous?"

He sucked in a breath. "So it was a man?"

"Not yet." An odd mix of anger and affection brightened her blue eyes. "And he might not make it to manhood before I kill him."

"Who are you talking about?"

"My younger brother."

He swallowed his sigh of relief, not wanting to betray how

jealous he had really been. Instead he focused on what she'd revealed. "*You're* teaching him to drive?"

She nodded.

"That's a mistake."

She tilted up her chin and narrowed her eyes. "Why?"

He stated what should have been obvious to her. "Because you are *not* a responsible driver."

"What I'm not," she said, the anger in her voice now, "is *her.*"

"Who?"

"Luanne."

"She was so bubbly and sweet," he said as he remembered her effervescent personality, "but also a little too irresponsible."

"I am not bubbly and sweet," Tessa hotly denied. "And I am not irresponsible."

"Yes, you are." He sighed. "You're just too stubborn to admit it."

"And you're too stupid to see the truth. You *want* me to be like her, but I'm not."

Maybe she was right. Maybe he did want her to be like Luanne so that he'd know not to fall for her. Because like Luanne, the risk of losing her would be too great.

She leaned closer to him, her blue eyes intent on his face, as her soft breath brushed his throat with her words. "Come *home* with me."

Chapter Nine

Tessa held her breath, waiting for his response.

His eyes dilated until black eclipsed the green irises with those distracting glints of gold. A muscle twitched along his jaw. "*This* is how you prove to me that you're *not* irresponsible?" he asked, his voice hoarse. "You invite me to go home with you?"

Tessa smiled. His reaction didn't disappoint. She'd expected as much. "I'm not irresponsible. I'm going to take you home to prove it to you."

"Inviting a strange man home with you is reckless, Tessa."

"Absolutely." She had been telling her mother that for years. "But you're not a strange man. I know *you*. You don't know *me*. You only think you do."

He slid off the bar stool, his long, hard body brushing against her. "So you want me to *really* get to know you?"

Heat rushed to her face…and other parts of her body. "I'm not asking you back to my house for sex."

At the same time, she couldn't deny that she was tempted. In his uniform Lieutenant Michalski was handsome; out of it, in faded jeans and an old T-shirt, he was sexy as hell. Thank goodness Amy hadn't joined the class at the Lighthouse tonight because she'd been pouting too much over getting assigned to a female officer for the ride-along, Chad would have had to fight the girl off.

But he wouldn't have to fight off Tessa. She really didn't want his body. For some reason she wanted his understanding, and maybe that was more dangerous than having sex with him.

His brow furrowed with confusion. "You just want to show me your *house?*"

"It's more than just my house I want to show you," she admitted.

"Why?" he asked. "Why do you want to show me anything?"

"Because you already have your mind made up about me."

"And you care what I think about you," he said.

She didn't want to care, but she was afraid that she did. Too much.

"No," she insisted to them both. "I just want to prove you wrong."

HIS BLOOD PRESSURE rising, Chad followed the speeding SUV through the residential streets. If he'd had the patrol car, he would have pulled her over, but he had to wait until he stopped his truck in her driveway. Then he thrust open his door, jumped down and slammed the door shut again with enough force to rattle the metal frame of the pickup.

"Damn it, Tessa!" he shouted as he stalked over to where she'd hopped out of her SUV. "You were speeding the whole way from the Lighthouse."

"I was *not* speeding," she protested.

"You were going well over the limit. I know because *I* had to go over the limit," he said through gritted teeth, "or I would have lost you." And he very nearly had when a dog had darted out between parked cars. He'd managed not to hit the poor thing, but the near miss had rattled them both. Or maybe he was only using Tessa's speeding and the dog as an excuse for the nerves rushing through him because he was here—with *her*.

"Ohh, Lieutenant Chad Michalski speeding," she teased, running her fingers up his chest.

His temperature rose as much from her touch as her mocking him. "That was stupid, Tessa!"

She sighed, pressing her hand against his chest, over his pounding heart. "Lighten up," she advised him, pushing him back with her hand before dropping her arm to her side. "I only went a few miles over the limit. You're overreacting."

"It was more than a few miles over the limit, and you know it. You should also know that those limits are posted for a reason. That's the safest speed at which the roads can be traveled." Without resulting in an accident. What if the dog had darted in front of Tessa? Would she have lost control and struck one of those parked cars? That was what had ignited his temper—the possibility of her getting hurt. Or worse…

"That's probably true, during the day, but it's late," she pointed out. "There's no one else on the roads."

"*I'm* on the roads."

"No, now you're in my driveway."

Realizing that he was at her home, he turned toward the ranch house, and caught sight of a teenager running out of a side door.

"Get the hell away from my sister!" the blond-haired kid shouted as he brandished a baseball bat in Chad's direction. "Get out of here before I hurt you!"

Tessa stepped between Chad and her brother. "Kevin—"

"Get in the house, Tess!" the teenager yelled, his voice cracking with fear and anger. "Call the police—"

"He *is* the police." She grabbed the bat from her brother,

nearly knocking the wood against Chad's head as she yanked it away. He covered her hands with his and directed the weapon down.

"You didn't get another ticket, did you?" Kevin asked with a groan as if he were the older, more responsible sibling. From the way he had rushed to his sister's defense, Chad was willing to bet he was. The kid glanced toward Chad's truck, then his clothes. "Oh, he's undercover."

"No, off duty," Chad said, pulling the bat completely from Tessa's grasp. "I'm Lieutenant—"

The teenager turned toward his sister. "Oh, this is the guy? This is *your* guy?"

Tessa tugged on the bat, trying to take it back—probably to use it *on* her brother. "This is Lieutenant Michalski. He's not *my* guy."

"Yeah, he's the one," Kevin argued. "That cop that pulled us over called you the lieutenant's lady. He must have meant *this* lieutenant."

"No, he didn't," Tessa insisted, pulling the bat free of Chad's grasp and handing it to her brother with enough force that it slapped against his palms.

"If he's not your guy, why'd you bring him home with you?" Kevin persisted.

"I brought him home to show him my family."

With a flash of disappointment, Chad realized that had been her true intention, not sex, as she'd assured him back at the Lighthouse. To prove she was responsible?

Kevin snorted. "Until you guys started shouting in the driveway, everybody was *sleeping*, Tess. You know how the little kids can sleep through anything. Or most anything."

A glance passed between brother and sister, suggesting to

Chad that they shared an old, painful memory. Something his shouting at her in the driveway had recalled for them both?

"I said *show*," Tessa repeated. "Not *meet*."

Kevin's young face twisted in a grimace of disbelief. "You don't have to lie about your love life," he assured his big sister. "I'm not a kid."

"No, you're not," Chad agreed. "but she's not lying. She really did bring me home to show me her family." He understood that she hadn't actually wanted him to meet any of them; she wasn't bringing her guy home to Mom and Dad. She was proving a point, and Chad was curious what exactly that point was. He'd been entirely too curious about Tessa Howard lately, like wanting to know what her lips would feel like, how her mouth would taste…

Shaking off the memories of their kisses, he held out his hand to her teenage brother. "So you're Kevin? You can call me Chad."

The teenager fumbled with the bat before shaking his hand in a firm grip. "It's cool meeting you, man."

Since he'd stepped from the shadows of the house, the floodlight from the detached garage shone bright on the kid's face. "You know, you look familiar to me."

The teenager pulled back his hand. "I probably just look like Tess."

Except for the blond hair, he didn't really resemble his sister enough to look familiar to Chad. "I don't think that's it."

Tessa stood silent *finally,* glancing from Chad to her brother, her blue eyes wide and watchful.

"Since everyone's awake, you might as well bring him in," Kevin said as he headed back inside the house.

"I might as well," Tessa murmured as she caught the door and held it open for Chad.

He stepped inside a warm country kitchen, where an older version of Tessa sat at a long oak table with a little girl on one side of her lap and a little boy on the other. The kids blinked away traces of sleep and residual fear and stared up at him.

Another boy, this one about ten, with a mop of dishwater blond curls, turned away from the window. "Is he really a cop?" he asked, his eyes wide with awe.

"Yes, Christopher. He's really a cop," Tessa assured the young boy. "Mom, this is Chad Michalski. Chad, this is Sandy Howard." She gestured toward the kids on her mom's lap. "And Suzie and Joey." Then she turned toward the boy at the window. "And Christopher. My sister Audrey must have already gone back to bed."

Five siblings, Chad tallied in his head. She had *five* younger siblings. An only child himself, he was awed.

"Audrey never woke up," Sandy said.

"I'm sorry about disrupting everyone's sleep," Chad said, guilt nagging at him. He had overreacted to Tessa's speeding. And his overreaction had obviously disrupted *more* than this family's sleep. His jaw clenched as he realized what kind of past experience his yelling had probably recalled—a violent one.

"It takes a marching band to get Audrey's attention." Tessa glanced around the kitchen. "And Kevin must have gone back to bed already."

"He pretty much ran through here," Sandy admitted. "But it was sweet of him to go out to defend your honor, don't you think?"

Tessa nodded, but her teeth gnawed her bottom lip, signaling to Chad that she was worried about something. Her brother? No. Probably about Chad meeting her family, especially since he had already upset them, however inadvertently.

"Kevin has been on this whole man-of-the-house thing lately," Sandy said, explaining why her son had been brandishing the bat.

So the teenage boy was the oldest male in the house. Tessa's father didn't live here anymore. At twenty-seven, why did she?

"Yeah, I'm sorry about waking up everyone, too," Tessa said. "I'm surprised you're home already, Mom."

"I take Wednesdays off now, so you can go to your class," Sandy reminded her daughter. Then she smiled at Chad. "I tend bar at a club downtown, so Tessa watches the kids most nights and usually gets them off to school in the morning—if I'm too tired after closing down the bar to get up with them."

Obviously Tessa had taken on a lot of the responsibility for her siblings.

Tessa nodded. "I forgot you have Wednesdays off now."

"Since you forgot, you didn't bring the lieutenant home to meet your mother, then," Sandy Howard teased, her blue eyes bright.

"Why'd you bring him home?" Christopher, clearly the most vocal of the younger kids, asked. They *all* turned toward their older sister for an answer.

Despite having a pretty good idea why she had, Chad turned toward her, too.

"I—I, uh," Tessa stammered, at an apparent loss to explain his visit.

"Why do you bring friends home?" their mother asked the younger kids.

The little girl whispered close to her mother's ear, but

the house was quiet enough that her words carried. "For sleepovers."

"You *all* have to go back to sleep," Tessa said as if she were the mother. "You have school tomorrow, and I don't want any complaining when I drag your lazy butts out of bed." Despite her gruff words, she tenderly kissed each child good-night, then pressed a kiss against her mother's cheek, as well. "See you in the morning."

"Are you spending the night?" Christopher asked Chad, undistracted by his sister's ploy to get them back to bed.

Chad bit his lip to hold in a chuckle at the tide of red flooding Tessa's cheeks. He just shook his head.

"Aren't you going to show him your room?" the little girl asked, then shyly turned her face into her mother's shoulder.

Tessa's gaze focused on Chad, and she nodded. "Yes, I'm going to show him my room."

Chad's chest clenched as his heart shifted.

"Ooh, Tessa's taking a boy to her room," another female voice rang out from the hallway.

"Apparently Audrey isn't sleeping," she said with a groan. "But you can meet her another time."

"Tessa's taking a boy to her room…" Christopher joined in the chorus.

Tessa grasped Chad's arm and pulled him from the kitchen, waving with her free hand at everyone as they left the house.

"So you're not going to show me your room," he surmised, ridiculously disappointed when he should have been relieved. He shouldn't have followed Tessa Howard home. The last thing he wanted was to get to know her better.

BRINGING HIM HOME with her had been the right decision. Earlier Tessa had had doubts about the impulsive invitation she had extended. Maybe that was why she'd speeded—just a tad, on the way home. *Okay, maybe more than a tad*. She might have hoped to lose him.

Now Tessa held tight to his arm, unwilling to let him go. "My place is down here. Be careful on the stairs," she said, tugging him toward the cement steps leading down to the walkout level of the ranch house.

The muscles in his forearm tightened beneath her fingertips. "Tess—"

"I just want to talk to you," she said, grateful for the support of his arm as a chilly night wind whipped around the house. "In private." Her teeth clicked together as she fumbled with the keys to her door. "Without freezing."

"You know if you dressed warmer—"

"We were in the classroom tonight. Not outside," she said. "I didn't ignore the CPA dress instructions this time." Fingers numb with cold, she finally managed the lock and opened the door.

Chad paused in the doorway, as if reluctant to follow her inside. Maybe he worried that she would pull an Amy and attack him. She flipped on a couple of lights before he stepped into the living area, which consisted of a plaid love seat and a white wicker trunk that doubled as a coffee table.

On the other side of the room was a wet bar, with a stove and full-size refrigerator. Tessa ran some water into a mug and popped it into the microwave. "I'm having hot chocolate," she said, still shivering but maybe more with nerves rather than cold.

His black hair glistened in the soft light. He was so tall— so handsome—that she worried a little that she might attack him, too. "Do you want something to drink?"

He shook his head as he settled onto the edge of the sofa, his focus on the pile of files spread across her coffee table. "You bring work home," he observed.

"I do a lot of work from home," she explained. "So I can help with the kids when Mom's working or sleeping."

"You help your mom a lot."

She stared at him, trying to analyze his tone for the censure or disappointment she'd heard from other men she'd brought home. She shouldn't care what Chad thought; he wasn't her boyfriend, nor would he ever be. "I try to do what I can, when I can," she said.

"It's great that she takes Wednesdays off," Chad remarked.

"Yeah." Tessa agreed with a smile. The microwave dinged, so she removed her mug and stirred in some hot cocoa mix with tiny freeze-dried marshmallows. The spoon clicking against the porcelain was the only sound in the room.

Chad cleared his throat and asked, "So what was class about?"

"We covered 911."

"Did you take any calls?"

She shook her head. "We listened in on a few."

"Anything serious?"

"A break-in. And an elderly lady who couldn't find her cat."

"Mrs. Huber?" he asked as if Lakewood was a small town instead of a mid-sized city.

She shrugged, reluctant to admit that she hadn't paid much attention. His not being there had distracted her nearly as much as his presence had.

As she joined him on the small couch, her hip bumped his, nearly jostling the mug from her hand. She set it onto the trunk, atop a file, to keep from burning herself. "I don't know who the caller was. Then there was a report of a woman on the pier, threatening to jump."

He sighed. "Probably Monica."

"That's what the operator said," she remembered. Tessa

also remembered all the calls for traffic accidents, but she refrained from mentioning those. "Of course, Lieutenant O'Donnell handed out ride-along assignments tonight."

"Well, I don't think you really invited me in to talk about the class," he said.

While she wanted to talk about the ride-along, about getting out of it, it wasn't something she wanted to discuss tonight. "No."

"You want to talk about your family," he said, but he didn't give her time to talk before he started asking questions. "Your mom is single? Your dad left?"

"Long ago," she replied, her knee bumping his as she turned to face him. "But I didn't bring you here to discuss my daddy issues, either."

"So you have daddy issues?"

She smiled at his interrogation. "No, he wasn't around long enough for me to develop any. None of the kids' dads were."

"So they're your half siblings?"

"I don't really think about that. James and Audrey and Kevin have the same dad."

"James? You have another brother?"

Her smile widened. "James is away at college. He got a full scholarship. He's a great kid—just nineteen."

"Wow, seven of you…" Chad murmured, leaning back on the couch as if stunned.

"The younger kids all have the same dad. My mom's not a tramp, she just has really bad judgment," Tessa said in defense of her mother, but didn't share with Chad her fear that she had inherited that judgment. Her point in bringing him home was so that he'd *stop* thinking the worst of her. God, she wished she didn't care what he thought.

"By bad judgment, do you mean she picked *bad* men?" he asked, his gaze soft with understanding and gentleness.

Tessa had never known much of either—from him or any of the men she'd dated. Her heart warmed toward him, but she turned away, reaching for her mug of cooling cocoa. "I don't think they actually started out bad. I think, what with Mom getting pregnant—she's extremely fertile, if you haven't guessed…"

He nodded.

"…I think they felt trapped when she got pregnant." With guilt Tessa remembered feeling trapped herself a bit more each time her mother had become pregnant. "Over time they came to resent her and even their own children."

"She goes by Howard. Did she never marry? Did none of the guys step up to do the right thing?"

She smiled. Despite being only in his thirties, the lieutenant was an old-fashioned guy. Or did that sense of honor come with a badge?

"Not my dad. They were in high school when she got pregnant," she explained. "He took off for college before I was born and never came back. She did marry the other two guys, but when things ended—*badly*—she took back her maiden name."

"So none of them help out with money or their time?"

She shrugged. "Child support payments come sporadically. They have new families, more responsibilities…"

"They have a responsibility to your mother, to their children." Disapproval and anger filled his voice. "They should do the right thing."

She smiled, amused that a police officer could be so naive in this respect. Maybe honor did come with his badge, but so should the realism that Tessa had learned long ago.

"They don't love her," she said, "and they probably never did. If there isn't love, there isn't enough to keep people together." She needed to remind herself of this, that Chad had already given his heart away. It—and him—would never be hers.

Chad blew out a breath. "So your mom has all the responsibility on her own?"

"I help her with that," Tessa reminded him with no resentment now. From Nana she'd learned that family came first. Over time and with the love for her family, she'd accepted that.

He stood up, probably as anxious to flee her as every other man who'd realized how little time she would have for him. "That's why you live here," he said.

"It's *my* house," she said, although she had never told anyone else who held the mortgage and the deed. Her mom had tried to get a loan, but too many years of using credit cards to buy groceries and clothes and not paying those bills on time had ruined her credit rating.

"You own the house yet you live down here," he mused as he walked around the couch and peered down a short hall into the bathroom and then her bedroom.

"I really want to talk to you about something else," she said as she returned her half-full mug to the bar and joined Chad near the hall.

"You didn't bring me here to prove to me that you're responsible?" he asked, his mouth curving into a slight grin.

"That's why I brought you to the house," she admitted. "That's not why I brought you *here*." She gestured around her modest apartment. "I brought you down here to talk about Kevin."

His brow furrowed. "What about Kevin?"

"You recognized him." Her stomach tightened with nerves

as she relived that moment on the driveway, catching Chad's reaction to when her younger brother had stepped into light. She'd just known the kid had been hanging with the wrong crowd and getting into trouble.

Chad's broad shoulders rippled beneath his thin, gray T-shirt as he shrugged. "I'm not sure."

"But you think you recognize him from somewhere," she persisted, not wanting him to spare her.

He nodded. "Yeah, I think…"

She stepped close to Chad. "Where? Where do you recognize him from?"

He lifted his hand to her face and ran his thumb along her jaw. "What are you worried about?"

She drew in a shaky breath and told herself that her heart raced with her concern for her brother, not from Chad's touch. "Kevin. I was looking for him in the park that night a few weeks ago."

"Why the park?" he asked, as he continued to smooth his thumb along her skin.

"I—I," she stammered, "I was trying to remember where kids hung out, drinking and goofing around…"

"Where you hung out?" he finished, wondering what Tessa Howard had been like as a teenager. Until tonight, he would have considered her a hell-raiser—someone who'd broken every curfew and pushed every limit. Until tonight, he had thought he knew her, but he'd had *no* idea.

"I didn't have time to hang out," she stated flatly. "I was at home—babysitting."

From her matter-of-fact tone, Chad caught a glimpse into Tessa's childhood as it must have been. Bleak and full of responsibility she hadn't chosen but that had chosen her. Yet he could detect no resentment in her tone or on her beautiful face.

She sighed. "So I guess I shouldn't begrudge Kevin hanging out and having fun, but I haven't seen, let alone met, his friends. And he comes home late all the time…" Her voice cracked with emotion. "I just don't want him getting into trouble."

"No, that's your job," he teased, trying to lighten her worries, now that he understood exactly how many she had.

She smacked a hand against his chest. "You're never going to admit you're wrong about me."

He caught her hand and held it against his chest, against his heart. "You were right. *I* was wrong. You're not irresponsible. If anything, you have too much responsibility."

"It's fine. Nothing I can't handle," she said, her chin lifting with pride. "I didn't bring you here to feel sorry for me. I just wanted you to understand."

"I do understand," he assured her, "that you want me to eat crow for making all kinds of incorrect assumptions about you."

"You can skip the crow," she offered, "if you tell me the truth about my brother."

He stroked his fingers across the back of her hand. "If I'd arrested the kid, I would know his name, age and address. If I had my eye on the kid because I thought he was trouble, I would know where he lives, too, and where he hangs out and with whom."

She nodded. "Yeah, you thought I was trouble and you always knew my name."

"*Thought?*" he reiterated. "Past tense?"

"You know better now."

He shook his head. "I know you're trouble now—even more trouble than I previously thought you were."

"Why?"

"Because I have no excuse to not do this…" He lowered

his head until his lips brushed across hers. Her mouth was so damn sweet, he groaned as hunger rushed through him, lightening his head as his body hardened with desire.

Her fingers clenched in his shirt, pulling him closer. "Chad…"

Chapter Ten

Tessa unclenched her fingers from his shirt and pushed Chad away, although her hands lingered on his chest. "I didn't invite you here for *this*."

"I know," he acknowledged, wishing he was relieved rather than disappointed that she had stopped him. She'd done the right thing whereas he hadn't, taking advantage of her in a vulnerable moment, which he figured was rare for Tessa Howard. He drew in a deep, ragged breath. "I better leave."

As he turned away, Tessa grabbed his hand. Entwining her fingers with his, she tugged him down the short hall toward her bedroom. Then, her palm sliding over his, she dropped his hand and stepped over the threshold. "Just as long as you know this isn't why I brought you back here…" she murmured.

His heart hammering, he nodded. "And *this* isn't why I followed you home…"

He had not followed her home to make love to her. Despite his best efforts, though, making love to her was pretty much all he had thought about ever since he'd kissed her.

"Are you sure?" he asked when she hesitated just inside her door.

Her teeth nipping her full bottom lip, she nodded, then

stepped back and gestured for him to join her. Now Chad hesitated. He hadn't been a monk the past four years, but those had been casual relationships. Nothing about Tessa Howard was casual.

"We're overthinking this," she mused with a shaky laugh, "when we shouldn't be *thinking* at all."

It wasn't the thinking he was worried about; it was the feeling.

"Don't worry," she told him, "I know you're not ready for a relationship."

"Tessa—"

"I'm okay with that," she assured him before he could say anything more. "I don't have time for a relationship. Every guy I've ever dated has gotten sick of having to share me with my family, so I've given up trying to find Mr. Right."

He studied her through narrowed eyes, as he would a suspect, trying to discern if she spoke the truth, or only what she thought he wanted to hear.

"At least I've given up on Mr. Right Forever until my brothers and sisters are older," she explained. "I just want Mr. Right *Now.*"

Although apprehension and desire tied his stomach in knots, he smiled. "So I'm Mr. Right Now?"

Biting her lip again, she nodded then held out her hand toward him. "You are if you want to be…"

"I want…" he murmured as he stepped inside the small room with her. The bed, king-size with a white wicker headboard, monopolized the space, leaving little room around the mattress. "I want *you.*"

A shiver rippled through Tessa, raising goose bumps along her skin. She was falling.

Then she was—literally—falling as he pushed her back and she tumbled onto the mattress.

"So you wanna play rough?" she asked as she reached out and snagged one of his belt loops with her finger. She jerked him down on top of her.

He caught himself with his elbows, and while he didn't crush her, his lower body covered hers. She shifted her hips, rubbing against his straining erection. "Oh, you wanna play dirty," he said.

"Actually I don't want to play at all," she said, partly because she feared she'd forgotten how.

He eased farther off and stared down into her face. "You changed your mind?"

"No, I haven't," she assured him, first with words, then with her touch as she yanked his T-shirt up and over his head. Her breath shuddered out at the masculine beauty of his chest—sculpted muscles covered with soft, black hair. Her hand shaking, she reached for his belt buckle.

His fingers suddenly covered hers. "You may not want to play, but we don't have to rush, either." He leaned forward and brushed his mouth across hers, gently nipping her bottom lip. "You don't have to always be in a hurry."

"No hurry," she agreed breathlessly as his mouth skimmed down her throat. She arched her neck. "You can take your time."

He tugged her camisole free of her skirt and edged it up over her stomach. She lifted her arms and let him pull the lace over her head.

"Tessa…" With his fingertips, he caressed the swell of her breasts over the cups of her flesh-colored demi-bra. "You're so damn beautiful…"

Heat flashed through her, her skin tingling from just the touch of his gaze, which ran hungrily over her. He reached for the clasp of her bra, but she playfully slapped his hand and reminded him, "There's no hurry."

He groaned, but Tessa lifted up and pressed her mouth against his. She slipped her tongue between his lips, tasting him. He groaned again.

"Forget what I said," he murmured.

"You don't want to go slow anymore?" she asked as she teased him with her fingertips, sliding them through the hair on his chest, following it down to where it arrowed under the waistband of his jeans.

"Hurry, hurry," he urged as he kissed her again with all the heat and passion burning her up.

She reached between them, unclasping her bra and her skirt and wriggling around until she'd discarded both garments and her lace thong. She reached for his belt again, but his hands were already there, pulling it free and unzipping his jeans, which he kicked off with his briefs. She gasped softly.

"*You* are so damn beautiful," she said.

"That's my line," he reminded her, his eyes dark with desire as he stared at her. "No, *beautiful* doesn't cover it. You're *perfect*."

She was afraid that he was—despite his demons—also perfect for her. If only he weren't still hung up on someone else…

"Shut up and kiss me," she ordered.

He lowered his head as if to obey, but skipped her lips to nip at her shoulder, her collarbone, then the curve of her breast.

She moaned and arched until he took her nipple into his mouth, laving it with his tongue. And his hands moved over her skin, caressing and teasing. He parted her legs and stroked her center until she shuddered with a climax. "Chad!"

She dragged her nails down his back, clutching him close. "More. Hurry. Hurry."

"Damn," he groaned and rolled off her. Pressing the heels of his palms against his eyes, he said, "I don't have any protection."

She flopped onto her stomach, reached under the bed and pulled one of her wicker storage baskets from beneath it. Hoping he wouldn't notice the dust on the wrapper, she pulled out a condom. He didn't need to know how long it had been since she'd made love because if he did, he might think this meant more to her than he wanted it to be. "I have some."

His lips skimmed over her back, from shoulder blade to shoulder blade then followed the curve of her spine to the dip of her lower back. "You have dimples," he murmured.

Her skin heated beneath his lips, beneath his touch. "Chad…"

He plucked the condom from her nerveless fingers. The sound of the foil tearing had her quivering in anticipation. She flipped onto her back and watched him sheathe his long, hard erection. "I know," he said, "Hurry, hurry…"

"You'd rather take it slow again?"

"I'd rather take you." He did, parting her legs and pushing gently inside her.

Tessa's body stretched and opened for him. "Oh, oh…"

"Are you okay?"

"I didn't know you were so big…" And that she'd feel so much.

He moved, slowly gliding in and out. Tessa shifted against the mattress as the pressure built inside her. She reached up, first clutching his back, then his butt—pulling him closer, deeper—when she'd thought she could take no more of him. He reached deeper inside her, touching where Tessa had never been touched.

Her heart.

"Hurry, hurry," she demanded, bucking beneath him as the pressure intensified almost to the point of pain.

He thrust faster—and harder.

The pressure broke, pleasure crashing through her. She buried her face in his chest to hold back the scream burning her throat.

Chad tensed, then uttered a low groan. "Tessa…"

He'd said her name. *Hers*. Not his dead wife's. Relief intensified her pleasure, and she came once again, squirming beneath him.

"Tessa?"

She closed her eyes, unwilling to meet his look—for fear of what he might see, of what she might reveal. "Mmm," she murmured.

His breath brushed her face as he leaned forward. Then his mouth touched hers, his kiss gentle. "Tessa…"

Unable to resist him, she opened her eyes. His gaze touched her too, gently. He kissed her again deeply, his tongue delving between her lips, just as his body was still buried deep inside her. She worried that he would forever be a part of her.

Suddenly he drew back—both emotionally and physically—and slipped down the short hall. Water ran.

Tessa slid under the blankets, certain he'd return, retrieve his clothes and leave. She tried to remind herself that that was what she wanted. All she had time for in her busy life was a one-night stand.

He walked back into the bedroom and leaned against the doorjamb, naked. Gloriously naked. She stared hungrily at his chest, his bulging biceps, his long, lean thighs. *He* was glorious.

Tessa's nipples hardened as passion reignited. She ran her gaze over him again, like a caress, and noticed that she wasn't the only one turned on.

"All you have to do is look at me," he mused as he stalked the short couple of feet to the bed. He pulled back the covers, baring her. "And all I have to do is look at you to lose my head."

Just his head, not his heart. That belonged to another woman, Tessa reminded herself, so she would protect hers.

He knelt on the edge of the mattress, and she shifted closer to him. "This time I'm going to keep my head," he said as if making her a promise.

"This time?"

He nodded. "This time we're going to take it slow." He reached out, running just a fingertip from her lips, over her chin, throat, the hollow between her breasts to her navel. "This time is just for you…"

He kissed her as if that was all he intended to do, taking his time, making love to her mouth. Then he made his way down her throat, to the curve of her shoulder.

"Chad…" she murmured. "You don't have to do this. What we just did…"

"Wasn't enough," he said.

"It wasn't enough for you?" she asked. Of course she wasn't enough for him; she wasn't the woman he really wanted.

"You were too much," he said. "I lost control. You deserve more. You deserve someone who will take care of you."

"I take care of myself."

"Not tonight," he said, pushing her back onto the tangled sheets.

SOFT HAIR tickled Chad's nose, awaking him from a deep sleep. Silky skin pressed against his chest, hip and thigh as Tessa curled against his side, lying naked in his arms.

His body hardened as desire coursed through him again. He wanted her even more now, knowing how good it could be between them, but he was afraid he didn't just *want* Tessa—he *needed* her. He couldn't remember feeling this way about anyone—not even Luanne. Guilt doused his desire. How could he betray his wife, the woman he'd vowed to love forever?

Until tonight, despite his physical attraction to Tessa's beauty, he hadn't thought he'd even really *liked* Tessa. He'd thought, because of her flirting and her practiced sales pitch and constant cell calls, that she was shallow and self-involved. He couldn't have been more wrong about her.

Now he had gotten to know her, more than physically. By meeting her family and getting a glimpse into her upbringing, he'd gotten to know her more intimately than he had when making love with her.

And he more than liked what he'd learned. He *loved*. Tessa Howard was an incredible woman: smart, strong and supportive of her family. Because of her family, though, she didn't have time for a relationship. He reminded himself that she didn't want Mr. Right Forever. Chad was only supposed to be Mr. Right Now.

She probably didn't want to get hurt if tonight was all they had, but Chad would, especially if they had more than tonight. He might start believing again that happily-ever-after was possible, even though he knew better. Even though he knew he'd already had his one shot at it.

Maybe from all his years with the department, or maybe from suffering the loss he had, he was too cynical to believe a person got more than one shot.

Carefully, so as not to wake her, he rolled Tessa away from him. Then, because he couldn't help himself, he kissed her bare shoulder.

"Chad," she murmured as she shifted restlessly on the mattress.

His arms ached to hold her again, but he tucked the blankets around her—to keep her warm without him. A sigh slipped through her lips as she nestled back into her pillow.

She was so incredibly beautiful...outside and in. His heart clenched as he crept from her bed and pulled on his clothes. He hated leaving her. Despite what she'd claimed, he had his doubts that she'd spoken the truth.

Had she really only wanted him for now or had she hoped to find that one guy who would stick around like her father and stepfathers hadn't? *He couldn't be that guy.*

"I'm sorry," he whispered. She deserved a man who could love her completely—who would be the man she needed. Chad couldn't be that man because he had nothing left.

He had given it all to Luanne and he'd lost it all with her. He'd lost himself—the part of him that had believed in happy endings. In love and marriage.

And he was glad that part of him was gone, he told himself. He was glad because he would *never* again feel the kind of pain he'd endured once. As he stared down at Tessa's beautiful face one last time, he ignored the twinge in his chest.

He was glad...

TESSA SHIVERED, cold despite the blanket drawn to her chin. The soft click of a door being quietly shut drew her fully awake. She blinked open her eyes to the encompassing darkness. Then she reached across the bed, to sheets still warm from his body.

So Chad had left in the middle of the night.

Well, at least she could honestly tell Christopher that the policeman hadn't spent the night. Even though she shouldn't have been surprised that he had sneaked out, tears stung her eyes. The tender way he had made love to her, then held her while she'd drifted off to sleep, had fooled her into thinking that a future between them might be possible.

Chad, with his sense of duty and honor, understood her responsibility to her family as no other man she had ever dated. But she and Chad weren't dating. He had never asked her out; she'd really been the one to pursue him. She wasn't the only one.

She wasn't worried about Amy, though. The college girl was no rival for Chad's heart. No living woman was because his heart already belonged to his wife. Despite her competitive nature, Tessa couldn't compete with a ghost, and she knew better than to accept a challenge she couldn't win.

Frustration knotted her stomach. She *knew* better. *But still…*

She had kept warning herself that Chad Michalski could only love his dead wife, but she had fallen for him anyway. She loved him even though she knew nothing could come of her feelings for him. *She loved him…*

The tears fell now, sliding down her face to soak into her pillow. She rubbed the moisture from her face, disgusted with herself for succumbing to such weakness. She hadn't wept over a man in years.

These were the last tears she would shed over Chad Michalski. She didn't have time to wallow in self-pity. She had too many responsibilities and too much self-respect to chase after a man who didn't really want her. Not for more than one night. Not for keeps.

Chapter Eleven

Chad pulled open the door to the pizza parlor. He wasn't sure why he had ordered food when he hadn't felt like eating in the three weeks since he had sneaked out of Tessa's bed. Starving himself hadn't worked when Luanne died; it wouldn't help him get over Tessa, either.

He also couldn't go to the Lighthouse because of the risk of running into her there. If he had to hear her sing again, or see her smile…he'd be totally lost, and he couldn't risk that again. He had barely survived Luanne's death and the loss of their baby. If he fell completely in love with Tessa and something happened to her…

Despite the deliciously tempting scents of pepperoni and garlic tomato sauce, his stomach turned. Maybe he would cancel his order after all. He tapped the service bell on the front counter. At the sound of the metallic tinkle, a familiar blond head popped up over the high counter that separated the wood ovens of the kitchen from the cash register area.

"Kevin," he greeted the teen with forced cheerfulness. Seeing the kid again reminded him of that night, of making love with Tessa. His face grew hot, which he wished he could blame on the heat emanating from the wood ovens.

"Oh, it's you," Tessa's younger brother replied with a lot less enthusiasm.

"Yeah, Chad Michalski."

"Pepperoni, sausage and green pepper stromboli," Kevin recited Chad's usual order.

"I knew I recognized you from somewhere," Chad said with a sigh of relief. "Why didn't you say anything when your sister introduced us?"

The boy's thin shoulders moved in a slight shrug. "I don't want Tess to know I'm working here."

"Why not? It's better than her thinking you're getting into trouble with all your late nights. Unless you're spending part of your time somewhere other than here?"

Kevin shook his head, then glanced toward the back where Giancarlo, the owner, sang in Italian and flipped pizza dough high above his bald head. "I'm working a few more hours than I'm supposed to…with school and all." Kevin leaned over the counter and whispered, "You're not going to rat me out, are you?"

Giancarlo turned, caught sight of Chad and waved. When Luanne had been pregnant, the pizzeria owner had been happy to satisfy her every weird craving at whatever hour. Luanne had treated pregnancy like she had every other aspect of life—as an adventure. She had dared to indulge her every craving, no matter how outrageous and unappetizing, and Giancarlo had always obliged her. Despite his boys being grown, the older man had assured Chad that he remembered what it was like having a pregnant wife.

"I can't get Giancarlo in trouble," Chad said.

Kevin glanced toward his boss and smiled with real affection. "I know. Everybody loves Carlo. My brother, James, worked here before he went off to college. Carlo even gave him some money for school." He turned back to Chad and quickly added, "But it was a scholarship, not charity."

The boy had his sister's pride and independence. "Giancarlo's a great guy."

"He's the greatest."

"Yeah, he is."

"But I meant me," Kevin clarified. "You're not going to rat me out to *Tess,* are you?"

Regret settling like a rock on his chest, Chad admitted, "I haven't seen Tessa in a while." If he were smart, he would keep avoiding her, but her ride-along was coming up in a few weeks, and he hadn't been able to talk Paddy into changing her assigned officer. Yet.

"So she was telling the truth," Kevin said, his face falling with disappointment. "You're really not dating."

He hadn't thought the kid even liked him, and he couldn't imagine why Kevin was as disappointed as Chad was.

"No, we're not." They weren't anything. Tessa's life was complicated enough. She didn't need a guy with his hang-ups, who would worry every time she left the house that she might not come back to him.

Kevin shook his head. "That's why I have to do this, you see."

"Do what?" Chad asked, unable to follow the boy's reasoning. "I don't understand."

"Tessa's so busy trying to take care of us that she never does anything for herself," he explained, probably not realizing how well Chad knew Tessa.

Ever since Chad had met her family, he had understood what her life was like and why she was always in a hurry.

"Except for the class," Kevin added, "all she ever does is work and watch *us.*"

"She doesn't think she's doing a very good job of that with

you. I think she'd feel a lot better if you told her what you're really doing," he persisted.

"I told Mom."

"She didn't think to tell your sister?" He really didn't get Sandy Howard. Tessa was obviously the most responsible adult in that house—and now Kevin.

"I told Mom not to, that I needed to do this. If Tess knew, she wouldn't let me work. She'd be like she was with James, making him focus on *school* and *homework*," he said as if those things disgusted him.

"That wasn't all she let James do," Chad pointed out, "since he worked here, too."

"She thought he was with his study group and that his extra money came from tutoring."

"Why haven't you told her that you're doing what James did instead of worrying her unnecessarily?" he asked, unable to hide his disapproval. Poor Tessa—she really had too much to deal with alone. He had foisted the class on her, too. She'd been telling the truth when she had said she didn't have time for it.

Kevin's face flushed, and he shrugged again. "She wouldn't buy it—not with my grades."

"Then maybe she's right, that you need to focus on your schoolwork."

"No matter how much I study I'm never gonna be as smart as Tess and James. But I am passing my classes," Kevin assured him. "Tess needs to lighten up. She worries too much."

That sounded familiar—something she'd accused him of. Apparently he wasn't the only hypocrite. When he'd first met her, Chad never would have thought he and Tessa Howard had anything in common. Now he knew her better—too well, in fact. He knew how sweet she tasted and how soft and silky her skin was. He wanted to bury himself deep inside her, so deep that they became one…

"It's time I was the man of the house," Kevin said, pitching his voice several octaves lower than his normal tone. "Instead of Tess."

"She worries because she loves all of you," Chad said, awed by the woman's capacity for love and selflessness. Her brother was right—she deserved so much more. Far more than Chad could give her.

"She needs to move out," Kevin said, "and get a life of her own."

So not even her brother knew that she really owned the house in which they lived. Still, he obviously idolized his big sister.

"Once I start making more money, I can help Mom with the bills instead of Tessa," Kevin continued. "I need my license first. Then I can *deliver* the pizzas. I'll make a lot more money then. Tips, you know." His face flushed with color, as he must have remembered Chad giving him tips every time he picked up his order. "Well, more tips…"

"You just have your permit now?" Chad asked, remembering that it had been Kevin driving when Tessa had been pulled over last.

"Yeah, and if Tess has her way, that's all I'll ever have. Mom's busy with her new job at the Lighthouse and the smaller kids. She doesn't have enough time to help me get in my hours, and Tess won't help."

Chad bit the inside of his cheek, refraining from telling the boy that he had just said he didn't want his sister so involved in his life. No sense in pointing out the teenager's faulty logic. Instead he sighed. "Tessa probably shouldn't help you."

"What?" the kid squeaked, abandoning his "deep" voice. "You don't think I should get my license, either?"

"No, I don't think Tessa would be the best role model for driving." Even though Chad understood her reasons, he still didn't approve of her speeding.

"I know," Kevin agreed. "She really needs to slow down. She's always in a hurry."

Not always. Images of the two of them making love, slowly and sensually, flashed through his mind. He held back a groan as he tried to suppress the memory. "Tell you what. I'll help you with the driving."

"What?" Kevin squeaked again, in surprise.

"I'd rather teach you myself," he explained. "It'll be better than your learning from Tessa." It would also save her from having to work in one more responsibility in her already over-loaded schedule.

"I know she speeds sometimes, but she's never been in an accident—well, except for hitting a mailbox," Kevin observed. "The roads were pure ice—everyone was going off in the ditch that day. She's really a good driver."

"She's a *lucky* driver," Chad said. Lucky that she hadn't been in a more serious accident yet.

"She's smart and not just about driving," Kevin continued his impassioned defense. "She was really good in school. She had scholarships. She could have gone away to college like James did, but she wouldn't leave us."

"You're right," Chad admitted. "She is smart." Since their night together, she hadn't tried to contact him, either. She had obviously accepted what he still struggled to—that they had no future.

"Well, she's smart about most things," Kevin allowed, "but she's not very smart about her own life."

"What do you mean?"

"She's dated some losers, like Mom has," Kevin said.

"Guys that wouldn't stick around, you know." He leaned across the counter again. "Guys that were really only after one thing…"

That was probably what she thought about him given the way he'd left. He cleared his throat of the regret choking him. "That's too bad."

"Now she's sick." Kevin expelled a ragged breath of worry. "But she still won't ease up. She's till rushing around trying to do everything herself."

Chad's heart slammed into his ribs, and his voice cracked as he urgently asked, "She's sick?"

The teenager nodded. "Yeah, must be the flu or something. You know Tess—she refuses to slow down even though she feels like crap. That's why I gotta help her. No one else will."

Chad could—with Kevin's driving. He wouldn't let himself do anything more than that. Just his irrational fear over her having the flu proved to him that he couldn't. He couldn't risk going through the hell he'd already endured.

A SOFT CLICK broke the silence in the dark meeting room each time the projector slipped from one slide to the next. Light flashed like the horrific images across the screen at the front of the room.

Tessa's stomach roiled at the quick snapshots of traffic accidents and suicides and murder scenes. The crime scene tech had warned them about how graphic the images were before he'd started his presentation. Amy had been smart enough to leave the room, but Tessa had thought she could handle it. She had never had a weak stomach…until she'd caught this stupid flu bug.

Sweat beaded on her upper lip. She closed her eyes, but

instead of blocking out the images, she saw them in her head. She could almost smell the blood, as if she were actually at the scene right now. Her chair struck the table behind hers as she vaulted out of her seat and ran from the room.

Moments later, the white ceramic tile cold beneath her bare knees, she crouched in the bathroom. The stainless steel stall door bumped her shoulder as someone pushed it open. Then gentle hands lifted her hair.

"You okay?" Brigitte asked, her usually husky voice soft with concern.

"I'm okay," Tessa assured her, now that she'd emptied her stomach. Again. "You don't have to hold my hair."

"I work in a bar," Brigitte reminded her. "I'm used to holding hair."

"Is she all right?" Bernie asked from outside the stall, where she paced like a mother hen with a sick chick.

Willing away the queasiness, Tessa stood up—with Brigitte's help. Her legs trembling slightly, she leaned against the cool metal of the stall. "I'm all right…as long as I don't go back into that room."

"*I'm* not going back in that room," Brigitte said as she shuddered.

The outer door of the bathroom opened. "Is she okay?" Amy asked, her stomach obviously so weak that she couldn't even come inside with someone getting sick.

"I'm okay," Tessa shouted, her voice getting sharp with impatience. "I wouldn't have even been bothered by those pictures, but I've had some flu bug one of my younger brothers or sisters brought home."

Yet she doubted it was just the flu that had brought about the queasiness. The slide show had reminded her of Chad again, that *this* was his job, the kind of stuff he saw. Then he went home to an empty house—no one there for him to talk to about what he had seen. He had no one with whom to share his life.

But that was *his* choice, and she wasn't about to try to get him to change his mind. She had enough baggage of her own without picking up someone else's.

"Okay," she said, summoning enough energy to walk to the sink and splash cold water on her face.

Bernie, having wetted a paper towel herself, blotted Tessa's forehead. "Oh, honey, you're as white as these bathroom walls. How long have you been sick? Maybe you should get to a doctor."

Tessa shook her head. "No. You remember what it's like with kids in school. They bring a germ home, then we keep passing it around." Sometimes for weeks apparently, although everyone else had recovered far more quickly than she had.

But then they were younger, and kids were more resilient than adults who didn't get enough sleep because they'd had to move to the couch to avoid memories of what they'd done last in their bed—and with whom. Even after she'd changed her sheets, it was as if she could still smell him, still feel him, his arms wrapped tight around her...

She, who prided her independence, hated the fact that she felt as though she needed him. Tessa Howard had never *needed* anyone before.

"Everybody decent?" a male voice asked as the bathroom door opened again.

"Lieutenant O'Donnell in the ladies' room?" Bernie shook her head. "I guess I'm not the only one who likes a thrill."

His sherry-colored eyes sparkled as he grinned. "I'm just checking on Ms. Howard."

"I appreciate all the concern, but I'm fine," Tessa assured everyone.

"Herman Schuster, the crime scene tech, gets a little too into his job," he said with a grimace.

"He's a ghoul," Bernie said.

O'Donnell shrugged. "Some people actually like his slide show."

"Then they're ghouls, too," Bernie said with a sniff of disgust.

"It wouldn't have bothered me," Tessa assured him, "if not for this flu bug I've had. As a matter of fact, I really don't think I can do the ride-along."

"That's a couple of days away," O'Donnell said, "I'm sure you'll feel better by Friday."

"You'd think, but I've been sick for weeks." More sick than she could ever remember being. Maybe that was due more to her emotional than her physical state.

"You should get to the doctor," Bernie repeated with motherly concern.

"I was feeling better," she said, "until the slide show."

"So I'm sure you'll be completely better by Friday," O'Donnell said, with little sympathy, as if he suspected she was only looking for an excuse.

He wasn't wrong. "But if I don't…"

Bernie shook her head. "You can't want out of the ride-along, Tessa. It was so much fun."

Bernie had enjoyed riding through back alleys and breaking up fights in biker bar parking lots, but Tessa had no desire to see any more of Chad's job—or Chad. Fortunately, her ride-along was one of the last scheduled.

"It was fun for *you,*" Tessa reminded her friend. "It won't be fun for me."

"You need to give it a chance," Bernie urged. "You talk her into it, Lieutenant," she said as she and Brigitte left Tessa alone in the restroom with the watch commander.

"It's not just the ride-along you need to give a chance," O'Donnell said as soon as the other women left.

"Chad?"

"You need to give *him* a chance."

"I already did," she admitted, hating herself for her lapse in judgment. *Mr. Right Now.* Really, what must he think of her for wanting a one-night stand? Apparently not much, since he had disappeared in the middle of the night and hadn't even called her.

"He didn't take it?"

When she shook her head, the lieutenant swore beneath his breath.

Chad had taken what she'd offered—one night, in which he'd taken her body but not her heart. That was good, though. She had no intention of giving her heart to a man who didn't want it.

"You really need to change my assignment. I can't ride-along with Chad," she implored the lieutenant.

"He's pretty desperate to get out of the assignment, too," O'Donnell admitted.

Tessa sucked in a breath at the flash of pain. Chad didn't want to see her again, either. Obviously that night had meant much less to him than it had to her. "So you understand how impossible it is—"

"I understand that you've gotten to him, Tessa. He hasn't really noticed another woman since his wife died…until you."

"I'd rather *not* be that woman, Lieutenant. I may be competitive in my professional life," she explained. "After all, I am the leading sales rep for west Michigan, but I don't compete in my personal life." Not when she knew she couldn't win.

O'Donnell shook his head. "You know, I thought you had more guts than that. I thought nothing would keep you from going after what you want."

"I don't want him."

"You keep telling yourself that," he said with a chuckle as he headed toward the door. "Maybe you'll even start believing it."

"I *do* believe it."

"Well, that makes one of us," he said. "You're not getting out of the ride-along."

"What are you doing?" she asked. "Do you think you're playing matchmaker?"

"I'm the watch commander," he reminded her. "I hand out assignments. I know who's suited to doing what and who'll work well together."

"So I take it you've been happily married for many years then?" She winced a little at her low blow because she'd heard about his nasty divorce. She knew his marriage had been far from happy and was long over.

But he grinned, unaffected by her nasty remark. "I know about *other* people," he said as he headed out the door.

"You're wrong about me and Chad," she called after him. Once she'd shown him all her responsibilities, he'd walked away…just like every other man had.

Chapter Twelve

Except for that one day when Tessa Howard kept him on the elevator, Chad had never been late for roll call. But he was late again today. Again, it was because of *her*.

He had been assigned to work the night shift because she was riding along. How could he face her after having never called her after they'd made love? What would he say to her? "Hey, sorry I'm a jerk like every other guy who's been in your life."

His hand shook as he fastened his holster, extra magazines, pepper spray, Taser, radio and collapsible baton to his belt. Thinking of the night ahead and how crazy he suspected it might get, he snapped not one but two sets of cuffs to his belt, too.

Then, angry with himself—and illogically her for putting him in this predicament, for making him care about her—he slammed his locker door and headed across the hall to the roll-call room.

"Glad you could join us, Lieutenant Michalski," Paddy lightly reprimanded him from the podium at the front of the room.

Still pissed that Paddy hadn't switched Tessa's ride-along assignment to another officer, Chad gave him only a short nod before heading to an open spot at a table a few rows back. Knowing she would be sitting in the last row, where the ride-alongs and interns were told to sit, Chad averted his gaze and dropped onto a chair. But his efforts were wasted, for she just ducked in the door.

The breath left Chad's lungs at the sight of her. She was even more beautiful than in his dreams.

"And there *you* are, Ms. Howard," Paddy remarked.

His fellow officers turned toward Chad, smirking, as if he had been late because he'd been with her. But he hadn't, not since that night too many weeks ago. His body tensed, wanting hers again. *God, you're a fool.*

"Please take a seat in the back row for the briefing," Paddy directed her.

Every man's head swiveled toward her as she walked down the aisle to the back. Even though she had dressed more appropriately for the mid-November weather, wearing gray pants and a black sweater, she was still sexy as hell. How was he going to focus on his job with her riding next to him all night?

"Oh, man, I'd love to be *you* tonight," one of the rookies murmured. "Hell, since she's your girl, I'd love to be you every night."

If the kid only knew how he really spent his nights… Chad was unable to sleep—hell, anyone who looked at his face couldn't miss the dark circles beneath his eyes, but only Chad knew guilt and regret caused his sleeplessness.

The watch commander called out district assignments, saving Chad from having to respond to the rookie's comment. Fortunately Paddy assigned Chad to the outskirts of Lakewood where things were usually quiet. Of course that meant he would have nothing to distract him from Tessa. Paddy sent everyone off with his final warning for them to "Be careful out there."

While everyone chuckled at his *Hill Street Blues* reference, they knew he was serious—he worried about them until they returned to the department at the end of their shift. Each one said something to him as they filed out of the roll-call room.

"See you at the Lighthouse, Paddy."

"Drinks are on you, Commander."

"Play you in a game of darts."

"Just not on Kent's board," someone else chimed in.

The voices quieted down as Paddy walked out with the last of the officers, leaving the cavernous roll-call room empty. Except for Chad and Tessa.

"Are you ignoring me?" she asked.

Chad glanced up from his computer. As he met her gaze, his heart lurched against his ribs. From the dark circles beneath her bright eyes, he wasn't the only one who hadn't been sleeping.

"I have to finish updating the files before we get in the car," he explained, his throat thick with all the things he really wanted to say to her. *I'm sorry. Please forgive me.* "We also have to get you a bulletproof vest."

What little color she'd had drained from her face, making the circles beneath her eyes appear even darker. "What? Somebody might actually shoot at us?"

"Hopefully not," he said, but he wouldn't lie to her that it never happened. Heck, from the video footage, she knew officers occasionally got fired on—even in Lakewood.

"But I can't take that risk," she said, "I have a lot of responsibility…"

According to her younger brother and what Chad had seen himself, she had too much responsibility. Was that the reason for her apparent sleeplessness? His stomach tightened with nerves and regret. *Or was he?*

She lifted her lips in a smile she might have intended as her usual sassy one, but it appeared too forced. "I really can't get shot right now."

Chad's lips tugged up in a less reluctant smile. "Would there be a better time?"

"No." Tessa sighed. "I tried to get out of this ride-along, you know."

"I know." He'd actually been surprised that she'd shown up at all. Of course, she wouldn't risk not completing the class and losing her license and her job. As she'd said, she had too many responsibilities. She needed someone to help her—someone who loved her so much he would do everything in his power to make her life easier. Chad would only make it harder.

"You tried to get out of it, too," she said, her voice soft with an odd note. Accusation? Pain? "Lieutenant O'Donnell told me."

"I tried," Chad admitted, "but Paddy's stubborn."

Tessa gave a delicate snort of derision. "He's delusional."

So she'd caught on to Paddy's not-so-subtle matchmaking attempts.

"I've missed you." He hadn't meant to make the admission, but the words just slipped out—of his heart, maybe his soul.

"Here I doubted you gave me a second thought," she mused, her voice sharp with bitterness.

"If it had been only a second, I might be able to sleep at night." The computer finished downloading, and he closed the laptop and stood. "Okay, let's go."

HE'D MISSED her. He couldn't sleep for thinking about her...

Tessa froze, unable to move, to follow him after his so

casually uttered remarks, which echoed her own feelings. She had missed him. So badly. She had thought of him. So often. Instead of being unable to sleep, though, she slept *too* much lately. Probably because of her never-ending bout with the flu. Or depression.

She cried so easily now. She hadn't been this emotional since Nana died. And she hated it. She hated him, too, for being the cause of it. When he walked back into the roll-call room, she glared at him.

"I know you don't want to do this," he said, with a heavy sigh, "but you really need to."

Or she would risk losing her license. She had come too far to quit now. Two more official classes, then graduation was all she had left.

After tonight...

Tessa had hoped he was kidding about the bulletproof vest, but he fitted a heavy black garment to her body, adjusting Velcro straps over her shoulders. Then his hands moved down her sides, adjusting the Velcro to fit her tightly.

"Can you breathe?" he asked.

Not with him touching her. Her lungs burned until he dropped his hands from her body, then she released a shaky sigh. "It's fine."

"It's still a little big on you," he said, "but it's the smallest one we have."

"Just another reason I shouldn't be doing this ride-along," she muttered.

"Am *I* one of those reasons?"

She lifted her gaze to his, losing herself in those deep green eyes of his. That was her greatest fear—that she would lose herself if she pursued whatever it was between them. She couldn't replace Luanne, and she doubted he could ever love

Tessa the way he loved his dead wife. No other man had ever loved her at all—not even her father. *Damn daddy issues...*

She squared her shoulders and answered him honestly, "Yes, you're the biggest reason."

"I'm sorry."

"For what?" she asked, trying to shrug but the vest was too damn heavy. "For not calling? For not stopping by my house or office to see me?"

"Yes," he said, the word nearly strangled by the guilt she glimpsed in those gorgeous eyes of his.

She shook her head. "I wasn't expecting anything more than that night from you."

"I'm sorry about that, too," he said. "You should expect more—you deserve more, so much more, Tessa."

She drew in a bracing breath. "I don't need an apology. I just need to get through tonight so I never have to see you again."

"If I could take it back…"

She nodded. From the way he'd sneaked out, she knew he regretted what they'd done. Until he finished his sentence.

"I wouldn't."

"What?" she asked, certain that she hadn't heard him correctly.

He leaned closer, lowering his voice, but enunciating every word clearly. "I would not take it back." His eyes darkened. "I would not change anything about that night."

Not even his leaving?

She ignored the warmth spreading through her, and reminded herself that she had been sick since it happened. "Well, I would."

Chad drew back as if she'd struck him. "I understand. I acted like an ass the way I left, not calling."

"I told you I didn't expect that, and I don't want to talk

about it anymore." If they did, if he explained or apologized again, she would forgive him—and then she would fall even more hopelessly in love with him.

"That's fair," he said with a ragged sigh. "Let's check out the car and hit the road."

Nerves fluttered in Tessa's stomach over more than riding with Chad. She hoped they'd been assigned to a safe area of Lakewood. She wasn't like Bernie; she wasn't looking for any thrills. Yet just riding in an elevator again with Chad had heat flashing through her body. The doors opened to the parking garage in the basement, and Tessa welcomed the cool, musky air.

Chad cursed under his breath. "They left me Pepé."

"Pepé?" she asked.

"Someone used this car to pick up the woman who probably started the oldest profession herself. She wears so much perfume that we can't get it out of the car," he explained. "You know—Pepé Le Pew."

She nodded. The skunk from the old cartoons that her younger siblings still caught on Nickelodeon. "You don't have your own car?"

"I do," he muttered the two words as if he was now the one reluctant to speak.

"And?" she prodded.

"It got wrecked a couple of weeks ago."

She gasped in surprise. "Were you in it?"

He nodded. "Yeah, it was a high-speed pursuit."

"You crashed?" Her heart pounding fast and heavy, she leaned closer to him, checking for scratches and bruises. "Did you get hurt?"

"No," he assured her. "But I had to stop the guy so no one else would."

He had risked his own life. And he'd accused her of being reckless. She held her tongue, unwilling to call him a hypocrite again. It wouldn't matter what she said to him, especially when it hadn't mattered what she'd done with him. He wasn't ready to move on yet. For her. Her only comfort was that he might never be ready. For anyone.

When he opened her car door, Tessa's stomach roiled at the overpowering scent of the perfume, which smelled like dead roses. The stench clung to Pepé's interior. "Can we keep the windows open?" she asked, willing her dinner to stay down.

"You might get cold," he warned her as he snapped the laptop onto the console between the seats.

She doubted that since she'd be riding next to him. "I'll be fine."

After popping the trunk button on the dash, he picked up the bag he'd dropped onto the ground when he'd attached the laptop. Emblazoned with *Lakewood PD* on black canvas, the bag looked like an overstuffed duffel. He extracted a clipboard from it, then carried the clipboard and the bag around to the back of the vehicle.

Curiosity about his job—about *him*—compelled Tessa to follow him. "What are you doing?"

Chad released a soft sigh of relief, grateful she couldn't ignore him entirely. He sure as hell couldn't ignore her. She was so beautiful but now, in the oversized vest with the dark circles beneath her eyes, she had an open vulnerability that touched him. That made him want to protect her.

"Right now I'm checking out the car, making sure I have everything I need." He had a feeling it wasn't the items on his checklist but the woman standing beside him that he really needed. "Since this isn't my assigned car, I have to make sure it's fully equipped," he explained, then pointed out the items in the trunk. "These long things strapped to the lid are road spikes."

She reached inside, her shoulder brushing against his as she touched the metal device at the end of the canvas holder. "This looks like a fishing reel."

"You fish?" he asked with surprise.

"No, Stepfather Number One did." She shrugged, "Or so he claimed."

"It's sort of a reel," he said. "Once you throw down the spike strips and the car you're trying to stop runs over them, you can reel the strips back in so the units in pursuit don't run over them, too."

"Oh, I hadn't thought of that."

"You missed the part of the class about the pursuit policy," he reminded her. "I covered it before the simulated traffic stops."

Maybe if she'd been there for his presentation, she would have understood why he couldn't pursue her. The risk was too high. "If it's a slow night, I can explain it," he offered.

She nodded.

His heart a little lighter, he pointed out the rest of the stuff in the nearly full trunk: the road flares, first-aid kit, biohazard kit, emergency blankets, fire extinguisher, police tape and traffic cones. "Here's where we put the video tape," he said, gesturing toward a black box mounted farther back in the trunk.

Some color had finally returned to Tessa's face, but maybe it was only because of the cold.

"Let's get inside the car," he said, dropping his bag in the trunk before slamming down the lid.

"What's in that?" she asked as she moved around to the passenger's side.

"Extra tickets." He gestured toward the book inside the driver's door. "In case I run out. Extra magazines…" He

checked the shotgun mounted between the seats, barrel
pointed toward the roof.

"Is it loaded?" she asked, her voice shaking slightly with fear.

"We have to be ready for anything…"

He turned the key, which they always left in the ignition,
and started Pepé. Heat blasted out of the vents, thickening the
scent of dead roses in the air until Tessa, turning almost green
in the dashboard lights, lowered her window.

"Can you press the garage door opener?" he asked, gesturing toward the one on her visor.

As she pressed the button, the tall door at the top of the
ramp lifted with a grinding of gears. Chad divided his attention between the downtown traffic and his laptop screen where
the computer sat open on the pullout platform between his seat
and Tessa. He tried to ignore her as she was now ignoring him
again, her face turned toward the open passenger window.

He couldn't blame her if she hated him, not after the way
he'd treated her. She had to think he had used her, just as she'd
said other men had used her mother. He could have told her
the truth, but he would rather have her thinking him a creep
than a coward.

The radio crackled, bringing Chad's attention back to the
only thing he wanted in his life now—*his job*. He listened to
a domestic assault call coming over the radio.

"Are you going to respond to that?" Tessa asked, her voice
cracking as she raised it above the wind blowing through her
windows and the heat out of the vents.

"What?"

"The call," she said. "Or isn't it in your district?"

"It's not."

"But you would go if I wasn't with you," she guessed.

"Yes," he admitted. He couldn't subject her to the bad

memories that just his shouting in the driveway had brought back for her family that night.

"Then go," she urged him.

"Tessa, it's a domestic abuse call," he said, which she had to understand since they didn't often use call numbers anymore. He turned to watch her face, and he caught the flinch she couldn't quite hide.

She lifted her chin with pride, and insisted, "You can go."

"Those calls can be really dangerous," he explained. "We never know for sure what kind of situation we're walking into."

"I *know*. I remember the video footage you showed us." Her throat moved as she swallowed hard. "And the footage the crime scene tech showed us."

He groaned, familiar with the tech's gruesome slide show. "Munster."

"What?"

"Herman Schuster—we call him Munster."

"It fits." She drew in a shaky breath. "But at least I know what to expect now."

"Then you know why I don't want to bring you," he said.

She sighed. "I don't mind not going, but I don't want to keep you from doing your job—no matter how dangerous it is."

"It is a dangerous job," he agreed. "We're careful, though." If only he had been as careful in his personal life as he'd been in his professional life, he wouldn't have begun to fall for Tessa Howard.

"I know," she said. "I'll be careful, too. In fact I'll stay right here in the car."

Believing that she would, he responded to the call. However, because he'd been outside the area, the suspect was already being loaded into the back of another police car when they pulled up to the scene.

He caught her sigh of relief that the suspect had been apprehended and cuffed. "You can get out if you want," he offered, "while we take statements."

She shook her head, and her face paled again. "No. I'm fine in here."

"There's no danger," Chad said as he stepped out of the vehicle. "You might learn something."

She shook her head again. "I know about domestic abuse."

He leaned back inside the car to meet her gaze; her blue eyes brimmed with emotion. Regret filled him over the pain she had endured and over the pain she obviously relived now. "You've been abused?"

"Not me," she said, "but my mom was. A guy that knocked her around."

"James' and Kevin's and Audrey's dad," he guessed.

She nodded. "He wasn't the only abusive one. The last guy she dated got a little rough when he was drinking. He never touched any of the kids, but he'd shout and throw stuff and generally shake everyone up." She sighed. "My mom has lousy judgment when it comes to men. Thankfully, after that guy, she's given it a rest and stopped dating for a while."

He suspected Tessa had had something to do with that, to protect her younger siblings. He narrowed his eyes as he studied her face in the glow of the dashboard lights. "You think you have her lousy judgment in men?"

"I've picked some losers. Guys who cut and ran." She met his gaze and held it. "I thought I was getting better." She sighed. "But I was wrong again."

"Tessa…"

"Hey, Lieu," an officer called out to him.

He ignored his colleague, wanting instead to explain to Tessa what he couldn't even explain to himself.

"Go," she said, "do your job."

"I'll be right back," he promised.

"Take your time."

He had blown his shot with Tessa Howard. Even if he could get over his fear of losing her and his sense of betrayal to Luanne for falling for someone else, he doubted Tessa would give him another chance. By leaving her the way he had, he had confirmed all her fears about men. He'd become proof of her lousy judgment.

Guilt pulled at him, more fiercely than it had that night. He hadn't only betrayed Luanne, he had betrayed Tessa, too.

Chapter Thirteen

Even though she stayed in the car when he responded to the calls they received that night, Tessa was excited watching Chad do his job. She knew he was the man she had believed he was: a man of honor who had the respect of his fellow officers. With his help, the other officers had obtained the statements they'd needed to take the domestic abuse suspect to jail. That wasn't the only call on which they'd requested his help. He'd also responded to a couple of break-ins and a fight in a tavern parking lot. Despite the hard time Tessa had given him since they had met during her traffic stop, he had *her* respect, too.

While he stood near the driver's window of the car he had just pulled over, another call crackled from the radio, giving an intersection for a traffic accident with "possible fatalities."

Goose bumps rose on Tessa's skin and she shouted through her open window, "Chad!"

"I heard," he told her, his fingers at the radio mike on his shirt collar. He waved off the traffic violator and headed back to his vehicle. "That's a bad intersection on the outskirts of Lakewood, not very busy, so nobody stops, and everyone speeds."

Tessa studied his face as he slid into the driver's seat. Was that the intersection where his wife had died? Tessa couldn't ask; she had been careful not to distract him from his job— but how did he do it? How did he respond to traffic accidents and not think of losing Luanne and their baby?

His jaw clenched so tightly a muscle jumped in his cheek, he focused on the road as he turned on the siren and the lights and proceeded toward the crash faster than Tessa had ever dared travel. Since night had fallen, she couldn't even see other vehicles—the lights just a blur as they passed them— sometimes on the wrong side of the road. She gripped the armrest with one hand and splayed her other one on the dash, not trusting the seat belt alone to protect her. In minutes they were at the crash site, the first unit on the scene. Chad parked the cruiser across both lanes of traffic.

A minivan had pulled onto the shoulder of the road, and the driver, an elderly woman, ran toward the police car the minute Chad got out. "Thank God you're here!" she cried. "Besides calling 911, I didn't know what to do."

"You did the right thing," Chad assured her. "An ambulance and a fire truck's on the way, too." He leaned down and caught Tessa's gaze. "You can stay in the car."

He didn't wait for her response, but popped the trunk button, grabbing something—probably the first aid kit, before heading for the damaged vehicles, which Chad had illumi-nated in the cruiser's high beams. He knelt beside the pickup truck that lay on its side in the middle of the street, inky gray smoke rising from under its crumpled hood. A car had hit the ditch, which on the outskirts of Lakewood were so deep because of the sometimes torrential lake-effect rains that everyone called them "suicide" ditches. The small vehicle had flipped over onto its roof.

Through the window she had opened earlier to combat the

overpowering floral perfume, she could hear cries of pain and terror. The voices were young. Thinking of Kevin and Audrey, Tessa pushed open the door and walked on unsteady legs toward the mangled car.

She never knew where Kevin was at night. He could be one of those kids crying out for help. With the cruiser's lights and some faint moonlight guiding her, she scrambled down the bank, over weeds and brush crushed from the path the car had taken. Briar branches tugged at her pants, but she pulled free. "Help's coming," she called out.

But Chad crouched on the street next to the pickup truck, assessing the driver's condition. Gasoline fumes mingled with oil and the metallic scent of blood. Tessa's stomach turned with fear and nausea. She forced herself to look through the shattered windows. In the glow of lights from the broken dash, she could make out at least five bodies in the car, but she couldn't tell for certain as limbs and torsos were contorted around each other and the car's mangled metal. There was so much blood.

"Help!" a feminine voice, weak with pain, cried out.

"Help's coming," Tessa repeated, glancing again toward the street. Chad scrambled down the bank toward them. "Thank God…" She moved, getting ready to stand up and meet him, but a bloody hand reached through the shattered driver's window and grasped her arm.

"Don't go," a male voice moaned.

Heart in her throat, she turned toward the kid, noting that beneath the blood matting his hair, the strands were blond and were eerily similar to Kevin's style. She knew it wasn't Kevin, but it easily could have been. She needed to help him learn to drive more carefully.

Was Chad right? Was she not a good example for her brother? With her speeding, she could cause a crash like this.

"I'll stay," she assured the kid, although she had no idea how to help him and his friends. Sinking to her knees in the ditch, she entwined her fingers with the boy's, holding his hand to offer comfort. "I won't leave you."

"Promise?" the kid murmured.

Biting her lip, she nodded. Then, knowing that he probably couldn't see her in the shadow of the car, she said, "Promise."

Chad moved around the vehicle, testing the doors. The window frames had been crushed, the openings now too small for more than a hand to squeeze through. Yet somehow he reached through the rear window, checking pulses as he murmured reassuringly to the injured kids.

Only a few of them were conscious, the others oddly pale and still as blood oozed from their wounds. Tessa clutched at the hand in hers, willing the kid to live. "Hang on," she implored the boy. "Help's on the way."

Then she pitched her voice lower and murmured to Chad, "Can't you help them?"

"We need the Jaws of Life. ETA for the fire truck is less than a minute." Sirens whined in the distance, but he continued to work from the first aid kit he'd pulled from his police car, wrapping bandages and tourniquets around the wounds he could reach through the nearly crushed window.

One of the girls inside howled in agony. Another awoke and began screaming hysterically.

"Shh…you have to stay calm," Tessa advised them even as her own heart raced with panic. Would help get there in time to save the kids? A minute had never seemed so long. She glanced toward the street and noticed that other police units had joined them, and a fire truck lurched to a stop on the shoulder of the road.

Relief flooded through her. "You're going to be fine," she vowed. "Just fine."

"It's my fault," the boy murmured, tears streaking through the blood smeared on his face. "I didn't stop. I was going too fast…"

"It's going to be okay," she assured him, hoping she spoke the truth. "Don't worry about that now. What's your name?"

The kid shifted, but as he was pinned beneath the wheel, he could barely move. He moaned, and his grip on Tessa's hand grew weaker.

"What's your name?" she repeated, trying to get him to focus on her and not his pain.

He groaned, his face contorting in an anguished grimace. "Tyler…"

"My name is Tessa," she said, looking over her shoulder as the fire rescue crew gathered their equipment from the truck. "Help's here."

"I…I screwed up," he murmured.

"Tyler, hang on to me," she said as his fingers grew limp in her grasp. "Stay with me."

One of the girls screamed again hysterically.

"Shh…it's going to be okay. You're all going to be okay…"

Tessa talked to the teens as she did Audrey when she worried about a bad quiz score or a hurtful remark someone had made. "You need to stay calm. I know that sounds impossible, but you can do it. You're young and strong."

Invincible. That was what they had thought they were, what Tessa used to think she was. Tireless and unable to get hurt. But they were wrong.

So was she. She had been tired for a long time, nearly nodding off to sleep at work and going to bed early. And she'd been hurt. Chad had hurt her.

He'd been right to leave her before they got in any deeper. He'd been right about her speeding, too.

She couldn't keep up this pace anymore, no matter how big a rush she was in. She couldn't do it for the very reasons she used to speed. She had too many responsibilities. Not only did she have to help with her younger siblings, but also she had to be a better example for them. She had to take better care of herself—physically and emotionally. She had to stop getting involved with men who couldn't love her as she deserved to be loved. Men like Chad.

CHAD HAD LOST HER. Instead of riding with him, she had ridden in one of the ambulances—still holding the hand of the kid she had promised not to leave at the crash site.

Tessa was not the woman he'd pegged her for when they had first met. She was fearless and amazing. She inspired him to be fearless, too, and stop fighting his feelings for her. He loved her. Completely. Hopelessly.

As he pulled up to the emergency room doors of Lakewood Memorial, he caught sight of her leaning against the dark brick wall of the hospital. He'd had to stay at the crash site until the tow truck came to remove and clean up the wreckage, clearing the area for traffic.

He had hated that she'd gone off to the hospital without him, but he hadn't been able to talk her out of riding along in the ambulance.

He parked the police car at the curb, and hopped out. "You okay?"

Her face was pale but for the blood she'd smeared across her cheek, wiping tears from her face no doubt. He shouldn't have let her get out of the car; he shouldn't have let her get involved. Obviously someone hadn't made it.

"Tessa?"

She blinked and glanced at him over the hood of the police car, staring at him as if he were a stranger.

"Honey, are you all right?" he asked as he walked toward her.

She nodded, but her legs gave way and she slid down the wall into a heap on the sidewalk.

His heart hit his ribs with fear, and he dropped to his knees beside her. He stroked his fingers across her pale face. "Tessa? Tessa?"

Treating her as if she were fragile, Chad lifted her in his arms and carried her through the automatic doors of the emergency room. "Help! I need help!" he shouted as images slammed through his head of the last time a woman he loved had lost consciousness.

Luanne had never come back to him.

But Tessa had to.

"TESSA? TESSA? C'mon, honey, come back to me!"

Chad? She could barely recognize his voice for its tortured quality. Honey? He'd called her *honey* as if he cared about her. As if he loved her...

That wasn't possible. The man was still in love with his dead wife. Exhausted, she slipped back into unconsciousness—or she tried. He kept calling her name.

"Tessa!"

She blinked open her eyes to a bright light, then winced and squinted.

"She's regained consciousness," a voice murmured from behind the light before someone turned it off. "Ms. Howard, how do you feel now? Can you sit up?"

Tessa focused first on the doctor in blood-spattered emergency room scrubs. Then she turned to where Chad stood behind him, his face tight with concern. Had she dreamed what he'd said? Had it only been wishful thinking?

"Tessa, honey," Chad murmured. "You scared the hell out of me. Are you all right?"

So she hadn't been dreaming. He did care about her. But then he had cared about every injured kid at the crash site, too. She would be a fool to think she was special to him when she had never been special to anyone else.

"I'm fine," she assured everyone, just as she'd had to at the CPA session when they'd shown the crime scene video. "I've just had this flu bug I can't shake."

Even though she was watching Chad, she caught a look of suspicion on the doctor's face. Her stomach suddenly pitched with a realization of her own.

No. She couldn't be…

"I think we should run some tests, Ms. Howard," the doctor suggested, his dark gaze intent as he met her eyes. "To be certain that you're okay."

Oh, God, she could be…

The doctor apparently thought so, but thankfully he protected her privacy in front of Chad, and refrained from voicing his suspicion.

"Isn't it just shock?" Chad asked the doctor. "She was riding along with me tonight, and was at the crash scene with those kids."

"How are the kids?" she asked. When Tyler had been wheeled off to surgery, she'd had to get outside. The waiting room had been too warm and stuffy and overwhelming with weeping parents and friends. She'd felt dizzy then and had needed some air. And Chad. She'd needed Chad. She pulled her gaze from his handsome face and turned back to the doctor. "How are the kids?"

Once again he didn't answer her. Maybe he couldn't because of patient privacy issues, but she caught another look on the young man's face, one of resignation, and tears stung her eyes. "I told them they'd be fine…"

She should have known better than to make a promise she couldn't keep. She had personally known the disappointment of too many broken promises.

"Some of the kids will be fine," the young doctor assured her. "Sadly some had too many injuries. We did everything we could."

How many families had been told that? She glanced at Chad's tense face. Had he been told the same thing when Luanne died? She imagined the doctor's words were little consolation for such a devastating loss.

"The blond kid," she said, thinking of the boy who'd reminded her so much of Kevin, the one whose hand she'd held at the crash site and in the ambulance. "Tyler, is he…?"

"*He* will be fine."

"Thank God!" She expelled a shaky sigh. "Just like I told him. I didn't want to have lied to him."

Like she'd been lying to herself for the past several weeks. Even before the doctor came back with her test results, she knew what they would be. She didn't have the flu. She was pregnant.

Chapter Fourteen

"So it was just shock?" Chad asked as he pushed open the door to his condo.

Legs still shaky, Tessa followed him inside his home. She glanced around the living room, with its masculine leather and dark wood furnishings. "It's definitely shock."

They had made love only one time. Well, twice but they'd been together only that one night. They had used protection both times! But the doctor's tests had confirmed it, though. She was pregnant.

"That's why I brought you here," he explained. "I wanted to make sure you were all right before you went home."

"You didn't bring me here for sex?" she asked, surprising herself that she could tease about it.

Chad's mouth dropped open in shock. "I—I—uh, of course not."

"That's good," she assured him, "because I really need to go to work in a little while." She had thought she would still be able to pull an all-nighter, but she had scheduled the ride-along before she'd become pregnant. Now her eyelids seemed to have gained weight, threatening to close.

Chad laughed, obviously noticing her state of exhaustion. "You're not going to be able to work until you get some sleep."

She shook her head. "I'm not going to sleep."

"You're afraid to close your eyes," he said.

Yes, she was afraid—afraid to think about what she had learned. Afraid that she didn't just have her mother's lousy judgment, but that she was *exactly* like her mother. Maybe if she told Chad…

But would he believe her? They had used protection. When the doctor had given her the test results, Chad had been with the kids, taking statements for the accident report, so he'd have only her word for her condition. If he accepted that she was actually pregnant, he would probably doubt he was the father. He would think she was trying to trap him just as her father and her stepfathers had accused her mother.

"You're afraid you're going to see the accident," he said, guiding her around a coffee table to the chocolate leather couch.

"What?" she asked, as she sank into the deep, soft cushions.

"If you close your eyes," he said, as he settled next to her and draped his arm along the back of the couch, "you're afraid you'll see the accident."

"Is that how it is for you?" She had wondered how he handled the job when she'd first seen those videos—and that was before she'd known about his past.

"Sometimes," he admitted.

She swallowed hard, bracing herself to ask a question that she realized might open up his old wounds. "Do you see *her* accident?"

His jaw grew taut. "Sometimes."

"Were you there?" she asked. "At the scene?" As horrible as the evening had been for her, she could imagine how much worse it would have been had the boy actually been Kevin, or if one of those girls screaming in pain had been Audrey.

Chad leaned back on the couch and closed his eyes. She noted the dark circles beneath his eyes, the lines of weariness in his face. She wasn't the only one who was tired to her core.

When she'd thought he wasn't going to answer her, or he had fallen asleep, he finally spoke, "I wasn't the responding officer, but I got there before the firemen got her out."

"How…how did you know?" she asked.

"She was on the phone with me when it happened."

"Oh, my God…"

"*I* was the reason she was distracted," he said, his voice thick with guilt. "I'm the reason she missed the light changing to red."

"It wasn't your fault, Chad. You can't blame yourself." But she knew he had been—for four years. Now she knew why the sound of the crash from the video footage had affected him so much.

"I don't always blame myself," he said with a sigh, "sometimes I blame her. For speeding. She saw the red light at the last minute. I heard the sound of the brakes over her scream, but she'd been going too fast to stop. She got hit twice, spun around and into a utility pole."

"Chad, I'm so sorry," she murmured. "And you saw the car…"

He pushed a slightly shaking hand through his dark hair. "Yeah. It was obvious she wouldn't make it."

"She died at the scene?" Tessa asked, picturing some gorgeous dark-haired woman lying in his arms. "But how did the baby…"

"They were able to take him in the emergency room. But he was too little. He hung on for a while…"

"But he didn't make it."

"Maybe he would have…if I'd put him through more surgeries. Luanne's parents—hell, my own parents, thought he would have. They haven't talked to me since."

"Your own parents?"

He nodded. "They didn't understand…"

"That you couldn't put him through any more pain," she said. "You did the right thing."

"Did I?" He lifted his shoulders in a tense shrug. "I don't know. If I had it all to do over again…"

She and her baby couldn't be a replacement for what he had lost. She couldn't tell him. "You have to let the past go," she said. "You have to let the guilt go."

"How do you let go of someone you loved?" he asked.

Biting her lip, she shook her head. "I don't know." But she was afraid she was going to have to find out.

"How do you let go of the pain?" he asked.

"I'm so sorry…" Unable to resist her feelings for him any longer, she slid her arms around his lean waist and laid her head on his chest.

"Tonight, for the first time, I didn't see *her,*" he said as his hands slid down her back and pressed her tightly against his chest. "I saw *you.*"

Tears stung her eyes, but she blinked them back. She usually never cried, so it had to be the damn hormones making her so emotional.

"I know I've been so stupid, speeding…like those kids. Tyler told me that he blew through the Stop sign—they were going too fast." Her breath hitched. "You've been right all along. I've been reckless." And falling for him had been her most reckless action of all.

"I believe that you've never gone that much over the limit," he assured her, even though his hand clenched her back. "I overreacted."

"I understand why."

"But I was *wrong*," he confessed. "You're nothing like Luanne."

Was that a good thing or a bad thing? She didn't have the guts to ask. She didn't have the guts to tell him about the pregnancy, either. She was too tired and too emotional. Afraid that she might lose control, she did the only thing she could. "I have to go. I have to get to work."

She tried pulling back, but his arms wound more tightly around her.

"I can't let you go, Tessa." He lifted her, carrying her into the bedroom. "You need to rest for a while."

When he laid her onto a soft mattress, she tried to close her eyes, but had a sudden realization. Her voice shaking, she barely choked back the tears to ask, "Is this…*her* bed?"

Her home? Despite her exhaustion, Tessa had checked out the modern condo and hadn't noticed any feminine touches, nothing to soften the masculinity of the leather furniture and dark wood.

"No. I moved here after…"

She died. Something broke loose in Chad's chest, as if, after four years, he had just finally accepted that Luanne was really gone. He wasn't cheating on her; he wasn't betraying her. *Not* moving on after her death, *not* living—that had betrayed her far more than his falling for another woman. For this woman.

Tessa sprang off the bed, her face still pale. "I can't lie down…like this," she murmured, pointing toward her snagged and dirty pants and sweater. "I'm a mess."

"You're beautiful," he corrected her, running his thumb

along her jaw. "So damn beautiful. Since the first moment I saw you, I haven't been able to get you out of my mind…"

Her lips curved into a slight smile. "I bet you just hated that."

"I hated *you* a little bit," he admitted, but not anymore.

"I hated you, too," she shared.

"Because I forced you into the class?"

"Because you're a bit of a pompous ass," she said with her usual sassy grin.

He laughed, unoffended. "How come you sweet-talk everyone but me?"

"I tried, remember?" She arched a blond brow. "You still gave me the ticket."

"Flirt with me now," he challenged.

"I'm too tired to flirt."

Guilt struck him. The circles rimming her eyes had darkened even more, providing the only color in her drained face. "You are exhausted. Lie down. Get some rest…"

"I really can't," she said, gesturing again to her clothes. "I need to clean up."

He lifted her again, marveling at the lightness of her curvy body.

"Where are you taking—oh…" She sighed. "Now *this* is a bathroom."

Chad set her on her feet and reached for the nickel-plated faucet of the deep-jetted tub he had never used. "It's a girly bathroom," he said, remembering the ribbing some of the guys had given him when they'd seen the place.

"The rest of the condo is all man," she assured him with a smile.

"I just use the shower." He pointed toward the separate stall. Like the tub, it had several jets, too.

While the water ran and steam filled the room, he reached

for her again, lifting her sweater over her head. He'd taken the bulletproof vest off her when she had collapsed at the hospital. Remembering how she had fainted with shock and probably exhaustion, his guilt grew, and he averted his gaze from her full breasts straining against the cups of a black satin bra.

"I didn't think of you at the accident because of your speeding," he said, needing to explain, to express his feelings.

"You didn't?"

"I thought of you because of how you handled yourself at the crash," he said, as he unbuttoned the waistband of her pants. His fingers, brushing against the warm, silky skin of her flat stomach, fumbled for the tab of the zipper then finally dragged it down. "How you handled those kids. You were amazing."

"That's what I've been trying to tell you," she said with a glimmer of her usual spunk. "I am amazing."

"You are," he agreed, then he reached for the clasp of her bra. The straps slipped down her arms and it fell atop the pile of her clothes on the bathroom floor.

She summoned enough strength to slide off her panties until she stood naked before him, swaying slightly on her long, bare legs. Every inch of her soft skin, every curve and dip, was sexy perfection.

He stifled a groan and helped her step into the tub. She closed her eyes and moaned as water and steam enveloped her naked body. He had to clear his throat before he managed to say, "Enjoy your bath. I'll be outside."

She caught his hand, tugging on his arm. "No. You'll be inside—with me."

"Tessa?"

"Don't you think it's about time you tried out your own tub?"

Tessa didn't know who she'd shocked more—Chad or herself—but she couldn't ignore the desire for him that burned low in her belly. She had to make love with him…one last time.

His green eyes darkened with passion as his gaze skimmed down her naked body. "Tessa…"

She tightened her grasp on his hand. "Join me."

"Are you sure?"

She nodded, knowing she wasn't above begging—if he made her.

He tugged free of her grasp and lifted his hand to the buttons on his uniform shirt. She knew that usually he'd go back to the department and change into his street clothes, unless he was covering someone else's shift. But tonight, or this morning, actually, he had brought her straight back to his house from the hospital.

She didn't want to think about the hospital now, though. She didn't want to think at all. So she began to hum striptease music.

A sexy grin spread across Chad's face, making Tessa's breath catch with how handsome he looked when he was happy. If only she believed she could really make him happy and that he wouldn't grow to hate her again for trapping him into a relationship for which he wasn't yet ready.

While she continued to provide some music, Chad played along, slowly unbuttoning his shirt until it parted to reveal a ribbed under shirt that molded to his muscular chest. He moved his hips to her "rhythm" as he unbuckled his belt and his pants.

She would have never believed she could fall for a man in uniform, yet she had. What was better was that she loved him even more out of it. He dropped his pants, revealing his hard thighs and dark briefs under which his erection strained. She whistled. "Oh, baby, take it all off."

His throat rippled as he threw back his head and laughed. "You're impossible."

If only he knew how *possible* she was…

He could have her if he really wanted her, but if she told him about the baby, she would never know if he really wanted *her* or if he was just doing the honorable thing.

He reached out, smoothing the line she'd furrowed between her brows. "Tessa…"

She shook off her maudlin thoughts like the water beading on her shoulders. The drops rolled down her breasts, and Chad chased them with his fingers, running them over the swell of her curves, then her nipples.

She lifted her hands to the waistband of his briefs and pushed them down to free the long, hard length of him. Standing beside the tub, he was at the perfect level for her to touch him with her mouth, siding her lips over the smooth tip of his erection.

He groaned and clutched his fingers in her hair. "Tessa!" Then he jerked back, pulling away from her. "You're rushing again."

She shook her head. "No, I'm done speeding."

He slid a fingertip along her jaw. "Good."

"You won't need to worry about me anymore," she said.

"I don't think it's possible for me *not* to worry about you." His hand dropped from her face. He then dragged his undershirt over his head, ruffling his black hair and baring his chest. He stepped into the tub with her, raising the water level so that it lapped at the rim and covered her breasts.

"Don't worry," she said again, not wanting him to compare her to Luanne anymore. "I can take care of myself."

"I know," he said, "but I want to take care of you."

Her heart clenched.

Then he added, "*Tonight.* You're exhausted. Let me bathe you."

He picked up a thick washcloth and a bar of soap, which he ran over her face, down her throat to the swell of her breasts. Tessa's worries eased as another kind of pressure built inside her, aching for the release only he could give her. He took his time with her, leaving no inch of her unwashed, even shampooing her hair and washing away the soap with a handheld shower massager.

When he was done, he lifted her from the cooling water. Skin, wet and slick, sliding against skin, he carried her into the bedroom. "No," Tessa protested as he laid her onto the bed. "I'm too wet."

His sexy grin flashed again. "That's good. Then I don't have to take my time."

"You're bad!"

"Your influence," he replied. "You're the bad one."

She sat up and wrapped her fingers around the thick, throbbing length of his erection. "You won't let me be as bad as I want," she reminded him, leaning forward to threaten him with her mouth.

He pulled back again. "No, I want to take care of you."

He did, pushing her back onto the mattress. As with the bath, he took his time with her, kissing every inch of her skin, making love to her with his mouth.

Tessa arched against him, moaning as waves of pleasure crashed through her body. Still, it wasn't enough. "I want *you.*" Nails digging into his skin, she grabbed his shoulders, pulling him up. "Now!"

He kissed her deeply. "I want you, too." His heart pounded against hers as his breath came fast and hard. "Now!"

She lifted her legs, wrapping them around his waist as she

arched her hips. His erection nudged against her. She shifted, trying to take him inside.

Chad hesitated, his body shaking with desire. "Wait! I gotta find a condom…" He rolled off the bed and headed into the bathroom.

Tessa caught herself from calling him back, from telling him it wasn't necessary anymore. It hadn't worked last time anyway. A cabinet door slammed, and he returned with a triumphant grin.

"Found one!" He tore open the wrapper and sheathed himself. Then he jumped onto the bed with her, wrapping her in his arms and rolling them until she straddled him.

"Yes!" Tessa exclaimed, the triumphant one now as she rose above him, then lowered herself onto his straining erection. She shuddered as he lifted his hips and buried himself deep inside her. "Ohh…"

He lifted his hands, cupping her breasts and stroking his thumbs across her sensitive nipples. She bit her lip and moved, and he lifted his hips. Together they found a rhythm. She leaned forward clutching his shoulders. Then he held her hips, lifting her and shifting her.

The pressure inside Tessa broke free, and she shuddered as a powerful orgasm devastated her. Chad shouted her name and buried himself even deeper, pulsing inside her. His hand shaking, he cupped the back of her head and pulled her down for a kiss.

"You are so amazing," he murmured against her lips. "We really need to talk."

She shook her head. "Later. I'm so tired." She wasn't entirely lying, as her eyelids drooped.

"I'm sorry…" he murmured, rolling and separating from her to settle her onto her side on the bed. "I didn't bring you back here for—"

"For sex?" she asked, managing a smile.

"Tessa, I really wanted just to take care of you," he insisted, with discernible traces of guilt in his voice.

She burrowed into the pillow. "And you did."

He pressed a kiss to her hair, then the mattress lifted as he left the bed. Tessa was asleep before he returned.

CHAD AWOKE to the sound of a door closing. "Tessa?"

He rolled naked from the bed, still warm from her body. As he walked into the living room, he squinted against the sunlight streaming through blinds. The room was empty, but he noticed the leather box that had been on the coffee table now sat on the floor, as if someone had been looking through the pictures inside. Tessa?

He had to talk to her, had to explain that Luanne was his past. Tessa—she was his future, if she'd agree to share her life, her responsibilities, with him.

Not seeing her in the kitchen or adjoining laundry room, he hurried to the front door and caught a glimpse of her outside, climbing into the back of a cab.

Was this payback for the way he'd left her in the middle of the night? Or was she just anxious to get back to work? He knew how much she thrived on her sales job; how she had not wanted to lose her license because she might lose her job.

But then she turned and her gaze met his through the windows—and he couldn't help but think that she was saying goodbye.

Chapter Fifteen

Gentle fingers stroked Tessa's forehead, rousing her from her fitful slumber. She blinked open her eyes to her mother's concerned face.

"Kevin said you stayed home today," Sandy said. "Are you still feeling sick?"

Misery and panic welled up again. "I'm not sick."

"I know," Sandy said matter-of-factly. "You're pregnant."

Stunned, Tessa pushed back her blanket and sat up next to her mother, who had crawled into bed with her and leaned against the wicker headboard. "You knew?"

Sandy offered a gentle smile. "I've been pregnant too many times not to recognize the signs."

"Why didn't you tell *me?*"

"I've known you twenty-seven years, Tessa," her mother reminded her with a little chuckle. "It's like Nana always said. Tessa has to come around to things on her own."

She thought of the car accident over a week ago when she had finally realized the true consequences of speeding. According to news reports, two of those five kids and the driver in the pickup hadn't survived their injuries. Poor Tyler had to live with that. She'd gone by the hospital to see him, but he hadn't remembered her. Thankfully he hadn't remembered anything about the crash, except the consequences.

She sighed and agreed with her mother, "Yes, I do."

"So you confirmed it?" Sandy asked. "Did you take a pregnancy test?"

"I had tests done at the hospital."

Alarm stole the color from her mother's face. "Is everything all right?"

She swallowed hard, choking down her misery and panic. "Yes."

Her mother slid a hand under her chin and tipped it up so that Tessa had to meet her gaze. "No, it's not. What's the matter?"

Her breath hitched with the threat of tears. "I'm sorry, Mama, but I don't want to be like you—a single mom raising her baby alone."

"I wasn't alone," Sandy said. "I had my mom to help me. Then I had you." She reached for Tessa's hand and squeezed it. "But, Tessa, you're not like me. You picked a good guy. He keeps calling here wanting to talk to you, and he doesn't even know, does he?"

"No." A tear slipped from Tessa's eye and streaked a wet trail down her cheek. She dashed it away with the back of her hand. "I want him to love me for *me.*"

She knew that was impossible. She had seen those pictures he kept in a box right on the coffee table. She'd accidentally knocked the box over when she'd been rushing out of the condo. She'd stopped to pick up the spilled contents—the mementoes of their life together. Their wedding album. Loose photos of many, many holidays and adventurous trips. They had been together a long time and had had an exciting marriage. Tessa had no doubt how much Chad had loved his wife. It had shone in his eyes and in his smile. Luanne, so beautiful with her dark hair and bright eyes, had reciprocated that love completely. Now Tessa understood why he couldn't let go of Luanne.

They had had something special. Something rare. Like the Gillespies, theirs had been a forever kind of love. It didn't matter that Luanne had died—nothing could destroy a love that deep and true. Tessa wasn't just competing with a ghost for Chad. Luanne was alive in those photos—and in Chad's heart. There was no room for Tessa.

"So you love him?" her mother asked.

She nodded, and another tear escaped through her lashes.

"That's good, Tessa," her mother encouraged, sliding an arm around her shoulders and squeezing. "It's wonderful that you've finally fallen in love."

"It would be," she said, "if I thought he could love me back. But he still loves his dead wife."

"Oh, honey, I'm sure you're imagining that because you're scared—"

"She's not imagining it," her teenage brother interrupted from where he stood in the doorway.

"Kevin!" Tessa hadn't realized he was there, listening.

"I was worried about you," he explained. "Looks like I had a good reason to worry."

"How do you know about Chad's wife?" she asked. "You barely talked to him that night you met."

Color rushed to Kevin's face, and he stammered, "I—I— I've been meaning to tell you—"

Fear rose with nausea into her throat. "Oh, Kevin, you haven't gotten into trouble—"

"No!" Both mother and son answered.

"I recognized Chad, too that night because I knew him from the pizza parlor," Kevin said.

Tessa nodded as realization dawned. "You're working for Giancarlo." Kevin idolized his older brother, James; she should have known he would try to follow in his footsteps, even to the extent of sneaking around behind her back. "You should have told me."

"You would have talked to Carlo and made him fire me."

She shook her head. "Just cut back on your hours. You can't work so much with school."

"See, Tess, that's what I mean—"

"She's right," Sandy agreed. "You need to cut back on your hours. School's more important than work." For the first time that Tessa recalled, her mother acted like a parent by setting limitations on her children.

Kevin nodded. "Okay. I'll be making more money now that I can get my license."

Tessa looked from mother to son. "You helped him get in his hours?"

Kevin's gaze couldn't quite meet hers. "Uh, no. Chad helped me."

"You've been driving with Chad?"

"For quite a few weeks now," the teenager sheepishly admitted, lowering his gaze to the carpet. "That's how I got to know him and how I got to know about his wife."

"He told you?" As a lesson against speeding? Chad hadn't even told her. If not for Paddy's interference, she might have never learned about Luanne.

Kevin shook his head. "No. He *showed* me."

"Pictures?" Those pictures she had gone through with such guilt at violating his privacy. Curiosity had compelled her to look through all of them.

"He still has their house," Kevin continued.

"No, he lives in a condo."

"But he still *owns* the house. He lives in the condo and rents out their old place," Kevin said. "He paid me to help him clean it up after the last tenants moved out."

"He kept the house?" Tessa asked, her voice cracking with hopelessness. Even though he couldn't live in it, he obviously hadn't been able to let it go. Like his wife…

"It's huge. Big yard," Kevin said, obviously impressed. "And there's this baby room that he doesn't let anyone who moves in touch. His wife did a mural of cop cars and fire engines."

Their baby had been a boy.

"It's really cool," Kevin said. "Christopher and Joey would love it."

So along with being fun-loving and vivacious, Luanne had been talented, too. No, there was no competing with such an incredible woman.

"Well, that's great," Sandy said. "He has a house all ready for a family. He's going to be so happy to find out you're pregnant."

Tessa fought against the tears stinging her eyes. "I don't want to be a replacement for what he lost."

"Oh, honey," Sandy sympathized. Pulling Tessa into her arms, she rocked her as if she were a little girl again, needing comfort after a bad dream. If only it were a dream…

She wouldn't have changed anything that happened except the ending. She would dream that Chad was desperately in love with her and wanted to build a life with her and their child. But he couldn't build a new life until he really laid his old life to rest. She couldn't ask him to move on; he had to make that decision on his own.

She would be all right if he didn't. She slid her palm over her still-flat belly, and happiness filled her. She was *pregnant*. She was going to have a *baby*. She also had her family, and she knew, just as she had always been there for them, they would be there for her.

"SHE'S NOT HERE," Paddy said as he caught Chad staring at the long table in the Lighthouse where many members of the CPA had gathered after class. Even the two female schoolteachers, who usually skipped the get-together due to their early mornings, had joined the group. The mayor's daughter, who he would have once believed had skipped the previous gatherings in favor of hanging out in upscale downtown clubs, also sat at the table.

Chad swiveled his stool back to the bar and turned toward his friend. "I see that."

"She wasn't in class, either."

She'd skipped the last class before graduation from the academy?

"She wasn't?" His stomach knotted with fear. Had she told him the truth about the results of her medical tests? Was she really all right?

"You're not freaking out over her violating the court agreement for CPA participation," Paddy observed, his eyes narrowing with suspicion. "She hasn't been in class since your ride-along. What happened?"

"You know about the crash—"

"I know about that. Fatalities. It was tragic," Paddy said with a heavy sigh. "But I don't know what happened between the two of you."

Chad shrugged despite the tension that had been gripping him since she'd sneaked out of his bed. "I don't know, either."

"Oh." Paddy nodded as if he understood.

"What?" Chad asked, his voice cracking with urgency. If his friend knew what was going on…

"She's been avoiding you? Skipping class? Not coming here?" Paddy asked as if reading items off an invisible list. "Not taking your calls?"

Chad nodded.

His friend offered a smile of commiseration as he said, "You screwed up."

"I did *before*. I thought…I thought I did everything right this time." He had brought her home with him; he had taken care of her. God, he wished she hadn't seen those photos. He'd finally put that box away, in the top of a closet where it should have been for a while.

"Did you tell her how you feel about her?"

He sighed with such force that his shoulders slumped. "No."

"You do *feel* something for her?"

She *had* made him feel again, and he suspected his friend knew it. So he told Paddy the truth that he'd barely admitted to himself. "I *love* her."

"You need to tell *her* that," Paddy advised.

"She won't take my calls," he reminded his friend.

"That's because you didn't tell her soon enough."

"Or it's because she doesn't love me back." She had never said the words, had never given him any indication of her own feelings. "Tessa is so independent and stubborn." And beautiful and sassy.

"You won't know how she feels until you talk to her," Paddy pointed out.

His shoulders slumped further as he braced his elbows on the polished bar. "She doesn't want to talk to me."

"So you're going to just give up on her?" Paddy shook his head as if disappointed. "You think that's going to make her love you?"

"You can't *make* someone love you, Paddy."

The watch commander nodded, a muscle twitching in his cheek as he clenched his jaw and acknowledged, "You're right."

"You can't *stop* yourself from loving someone, either," Chad realized. He dropped some money on the bar. "I'll see you tomorrow."

"I bet you're going to see someone else tonight."

"I have to tell her how I feel…even if she doesn't feel the same."

"Good luck."

He nodded in acceptance, suspecting he would need luck. As he'd said, Tessa was stubborn.

A short while later, he gave up knocking on the sliding glass doors of the basement apartment. He couldn't yell and risk waking up and scaring her family again.

"Hey," Kevin called down from the driveway where he leaned against Tessa's SUV, his baseball bat at his side.

"She's home," Chad said, gesturing toward her vehicle as he climbed the cement steps to join the kid. "But she won't answer her door."

"Why do you want to see her?" the teenager asked, then tossed his words back at him. "I thought you two weren't anything to each other."

While teaching him to drive over the past several weeks, Chad had gotten to know Kevin. Chad had even thought they'd gotten kind of close, but now he detected a belligerence in the boy's tone.

"She missed class," he said, unwilling to share his real reason until he'd spoken to Tessa. "Not the first time she's missed class, either. She's violating her agreement with the traffic court judge. She'll probably lose her license."

"So?" Kevin shrugged his thin shoulders. "If she does, I'll drive her around. Mom's going to let me get my license this week."

"That's great."

Some of the tension eased from the kid, and he flashed a smile. "Thanks for your help."

Chad shrugged off the kid's gratitude. He hadn't helped Kevin for his sake. He had helped him to relieve Tessa of one of her too many responsibilities.

"So tell me—why isn't she answering her door?" Chad persisted.

The belligerence returned, twisting Kevin's mouth into a sarcastic grin. "I would guess that she doesn't want to talk to you."

"Okay." Frustration frayed Chad's nerves. The woman was so damn stubborn. Too stubborn to give them a chance? Was he wasting his time?

Kevin sighed. "Or she's sick again."

Concern replaced his frustration. "Did she get the flu back?"

Kevin shook his head, tumbling his blond hair into his eyes. "It's not the flu."

Fear pressed hard on Chad's chest, stealing away his breath. "What's wrong with her?"

"Morning sickness. Or in Tess's case, all-day sickness," Kevin said with sympathy even as he grimaced in disgust. "She's pretty miserable."

"She's *pregnant?*"

Kevin nodded again.

Shocked, Chad expelled a ragged sigh. "She knew since that day at the hospital, didn't she? She knew and she didn't tell me."

Not only that but she'd been avoiding him.

God, he had a right to know. Anger gripped him so tightly that he couldn't think, he couldn't speak. He whirled away from her vehicle and stalked to his truck. He couldn't talk to her now, not when she was sick and he was so damned pissed he could hardly see straight.

Chapter Sixteen

"Kevin!" Tessa yelled at her brother as she pulled open the sliding glass door where she'd been straining to eavesdrop. "Why'd you tell him?"

Kevin shrugged. "I didn't know it was supposed to be a secret."

Tires squealed against asphalt as Chad's truck peeled out of the driveway. "I have to talk to him."

"I can drive you," Kevin offered. "Chad taught me to be a real good driver."

She'd heard Kevin's thank-you. Despite their lowered voices, she had caught every word of their conversation and every rap of Chad's knuckles against her door. But she'd ignored him. She couldn't ignore him anymore. She had to stop being a coward.

Grabbing her keys from inside, she ran up the steps and jumped into her SUV.

Chad had slowed down slightly, but he was still driving too fast when she caught up with him by the park. She flashed her lights—on and off, on and off—and tooted her horn until he finally pulled to the curb. She jumped down from her vehicle and ran up to his, then knocked on his window.

He rolled it down with a warning, "You don't want to talk to me right now." His deep voice vibrated with anger.

"Chad—"

"You've been avoiding me for weeks. Now I understand why."

"It's your baby," she said.

His brows furrowed. "Of course it is."

Just like that, he had allayed one of her fears. Avoiding him had been foolish, she realized now. Even though he was furious with her, he wasn't hurtful. She curled her fingers around his window frame. "Do you know how fast you were going?" she asked.

He blinked, probably unable to follow her change of subject. "I don't know."

"I *know*. You were going at least five, maybe ten, miles over the limit," she scolded.

He grimaced, but then a slight grin lifted his mouth. "There's no one else on the roads right now."

"*I'm* on the roads right now."

He opened his door and stepped out of the truck, then leaned against the side of the pickup cab. "Why'd you come after me if you didn't want me to know about the baby?"

"It's not that I didn't want you to know," she said. "I was afraid to tell you."

"Why?" His face paled in the glow of the street lamp. "Don't you want to keep it?"

She placed her hands over her stomach protectively. "I do." At first she'd been overwhelmed, but now she looked forward to having a child, to having *Chad's* child.

"Then why not talk to me?" he asked.

"I didn't think you were ready," she admitted, "to move

on. I know how much you loved your wife—how much you still love her."

"I lost Luanne, but that was out of my control. It wasn't my fault," he said, almost as if he really believed what he was saying.

"No, it wasn't," she agreed. "You have to stop feeling guilty over her death."

"I have," he insisted, "*because* of you."

She believed that he had finally let go of his guilt, but she wasn't convinced she had had any part in it. "I'm glad."

"If I lose you, though," he said, "that *will* be my fault."

"You can't control me," she warned him, worried that he wouldn't trust her to drive, that he'd want to take away her independence now that he knew she carried his child.

"I know," he said. "You're fiercely independent." He grinned, "And stubborn."

Unoffended since he spoke the truth, she nodded.

"That's why I fought so hard against falling for you," he explained.

Her heart warmed with hope. "Are you still fighting?"

"I stopped fighting my feelings the night of the ride-along. I was going to tell you how I felt when you woke up, but you disappeared on me," he said, his deep voice rough with emotion.

The last thing she'd wanted to do was hurt him; the man had already endured too much pain.

"I was in shock," she explained. "From the accident, but also from finding out I'm pregnant."

His hands, shaking slightly, covered hers on her stomach. "I'm in shock, too. We used protection."

"I know," she said with a sigh, still surprised it hadn't been effective. "That's why I didn't know if you'd believe me."

His brow furrowed. "Why wouldn't I?"

She shrugged. "You might think that I was like my mother."

"You're not like your mother, Tessa." He squeezed her hands. "You have better taste in men, for one thing."

She smiled and teased, "I wasn't so sure about that."

"I've been a jerk," he said, his eyes dark with regret.

"You weren't alone in acting that way," she admitted. "I'm sorry I've been avoiding you."

"I'll talk to Paddy and the judge about the classes you've missed," he assured her. "I'll make sure that you don't get in trouble with the traffic court."

"You don't have to take care of me."

"I know I don't *have* to," he said. "You've been taking care of yourself and everyone you care about for a long time on your own. But I want to take care of *you* now." He tipped up her chin so her gaze met his serious, intent one. "I want to marry you."

She wanted to throw her arms around his neck and shout her acceptance, but she couldn't risk the disappointment and the pain that might follow if she didn't know the truth. "Why?"

He stared down at her, his green eyes glittering in the glow from the street lamp. "Because I love you."

She wanted to believe him, but she remembered those photos and Kevin's description of that house.

"Would you want to marry me *now,*" she asked, her heart aching with the question and with fear of his response, but she had to know. "Would you love me if I wasn't pregnant?"

"I started falling for you that first time I pulled you over," he professed.

"I thought my flirting didn't affect you," she reminded him.

Chad grinned. "I lied."

She couldn't help but think he was lying now about his love so that she would let him do the honorable thing.

"You brought me back to life."

"I don't want to be a replacement for Luanne," she said with panic, and she pressed her fingers protectively against her belly. "I don't want *my* baby to be a replacement for the one you lost."

He entwined his fingers with hers. "*Our* baby. And you could never replace Luanne."

She closed her eyes against the threat of tears at his words. "This is why I fought my feelings for you," she murmured. "Because I knew you could never love me as much as you loved her…"

Realizing he'd hurt her, Chad shook his head. He cupped her face, tipping up her chin so that she opened her eyes and met his gaze. "You don't understand—"

"I saw the pictures," she interrupted. "I saw how much you loved her. If she hadn't died, we wouldn't be here. Together. You'd be with her, happier than I could ever make you."

"Tessa, that's not fair," he said. "What if one of those guys you'd gone out with had stuck around, had loved you like you deserved to be loved?"

"But I didn't love any of them."

His heart lifted with hope. Could she—did she—*love* him? "Just because I loved Luanne doesn't mean I can't love you, too," he insisted, trying to make her understand what he had struggled so long to accept.

"You married *her* because you loved her. You want to marry me because I'm pregnant." Her voice trembled with the threat of sobs. "Eventually you'll come to resent and hate me—"

"I could never resent you and hate you."

"You already have," she reminded him.

He sighed. "God, you're stubborn."

"And right…"

"I hated you for making me feel again," he admitted. "I resented you for making me love you. I loved you *before* I knew you were pregnant. And I'll love you forever."

Tessa dashed away tears with the back of her hand. "I know about the house. Kevin told me. About her mural in the baby's room. If I say yes, will you move me and the baby in there as your replacement family?"

"You can't replace her," Chad said again, and as Tessa drew in a sharp breath, he wrapped his arms around her, "because you're *nothing* alike. What I felt for Luanne is completely different from what I feel for you. Luanne is my past."

He suspected Luanne would be happy that he could finally leave her there, that he could finally let her go and live again. Luanne had been all about living.

"Tessa, you are my future," he declared, "if you'll stop fighting your feelings for me."

Tears streaking her face, she nodded. "I stopped during the ride-along. Watching you do your job, seeing what kind of man you are, I knew I couldn't help myself anymore. I was in too deep."

"That's another reason you've been avoiding me," he realized.

"Because I love you so much, you could hurt me so badly if you didn't return my feelings," she sniffed, her voice betraying her vulnerability.

He cupped her beautiful face in his hands and lowered his head until his lips brushed across hers. "I'm sorry I took so long to realize how much I love you. Hell, I *knew*—I was just too scared to *admit* how much I love you."

"You really do?" she asked, her eyes damp with tears and wide with awe as if she still struggled to believe him.

"I don't want to move you into my old house," he insisted,

trying to allay all her fear and doubts. "I'm ready to sell it now, to let go of every part of the past."

"I don't want you to forget about Luanne," she assured him. "I don't want you not to love her anymore. I just want you to love me—*really* love me, too."

He nodded, so glad she understood. "She was my first love. You're my last love."

She sighed with relief as if she finally let go of all her doubts. Then she smiled and said, "I might have a buyer for your house."

"You're not in real-estate sales," he reminded her.

"But I know the perfect family for it. Mine," she suggested. "My mom and the kids."

He nodded. "That's great. Then I can move into your house because I don't want to spend another minute apart from you."

Her mouth curved into that sassy smile that had drawn him in the first moment he'd met her. She asked, "You want me to ride along again?"

"I want you to ride along with me for the rest of our lives." He knelt right there, in the street, next to their vehicles and proposed. "Will you marry me?"

"Yes." She threw her arms around his neck and held on tight. "I love you so much!"

"I love you…"

A siren squawked and lights flashed as a police car pulled up next to them. The window rolled down, and a familiar, deep voice asked, "Everything all right here?"

Chad grinned at his friend and colleague. "Everything's *perfect* here, Paddy."

Tessa could not have agreed more. Brimming with happiness,

she leaned over to peer inside the car. The watch commander wasn't out on patrol alone. Erin Powell sat in the passenger's seat, her notebook open across her lap. Her eyes sparkled with unshed tears as she smiled up at Tessa. "Congratulations," she said, obviously understanding that Chad had proposed.

As the two drove off, Tessa turned back to her fiancé. "Well, our secret's out," she mused.

"I don't intend to keep my feelings a secret anymore," Chad promised. "I want the world to know how I feel about you."

She smiled, her heart full with her love for this man—and his love for her. "I doubt we'll get mentioned in Erin's column in the *Chronicle*."

He shrugged. "Then we'll have to put in our own announcement of our engagement."

Her happiness brimmed over. "I know you've done the big wedding before," she said, remembering—without any jealousy this time—the photos from his ceremony with Luanne. "But with my family and the other members of the citizens' police academy…"

"And the entire department," Chad added with a grin. "We're going to have to have a big wedding."

"You don't mind?" she asked, knowing and accepting that Chad would always have some painful memories. But they—and Luanne's love—had made him the man Tessa loved.

"Not at all. I have only one stipulation about the wedding," he said.

She gazed up at him, at the love flowing from his beautiful eyes, glinting in those flecks of gold. "And that is?"

"That we hurry! I want you to be my wife as soon as possible."

She rose on tiptoe and pressed a kiss against his sexy mouth. "Too bad we hadn't gotten this on tape," she murmured against his lips.

"What?"

"Lieutenant Chad Michalski urging me to speed…" She slid her mouth across his, savoring the sweetness of the kiss. "But there's no reason to rush," she assured him.

He kissed her back. "We have the rest of our lives."

* * * * *

There's more love to be found within the
Lakewood Citizens' Police Academy!
Watch for Lisa Childs' next book in the miniseries.
ONCE A HERO, coming May 2009,
only from Harlequin American Romance!

Harlequin is 60 years old,
and Harlequin Blaze is celebrating!
After all, a lot can happen in 60 years,
or 60 minutes…or 60 seconds!
Find out what's going down in Blaze's
heart-stopping new mini-series,
FROM 0 TO 60!
Getting from "Hello" to "How was it?"
can happen fast….

Here's a sneak peek of the first book,
A LONG, HARD RIDE
by Alison Kent
Available March 2009.

"Is that for me?" Trey asked.

Cardin Worth cocked her head to the side and considered how much better the day already seemed. "Good morning to you, too."

When she didn't hold out the second cup of coffee for him to take, he came closer. She sipped from her heavy white mug, hiding her grin and her giddy rush of nerves behind it.

But when he stopped in front of her, she made the mistake of lowering her gaze from his face to the exposed strip of his chest. It was either give him his cup of coffee or bury her nose against him and breathe in. She remembered so clearly how he smelled. How he tasted.

She gave him his coffee.

After taking a quick gulp, he smiled and said, "Good morning, Cardin. I hope the floor wasn't too hard for you."

The hardness of the floor hadn't been the problem. She shook her head. "Are you kidding? I slept like a baby, swaddled in my sleeping bag."

"In my sleeping bag, you mean."

If he wanted to get technical, yeah. "Thanks for the loaner. It made sleeping on the floor almost bearable." As had the warmth of his spooned body, she thought, then quickly changed the subject. "I saw you have a loaf of bread and some eggs. Would you like me to cook breakfast?"

He lowered his coffee mug slowly, his gaze as warm as the sun on her shoulders, as the ceramic heating her hands. "I didn't bring you out here to wait on me."

"You didn't bring me out here at all. I volunteered to come."

"To help me get ready for the race. Not to serve me."

"It's just breakfast, Trey. And coffee." Even if last night it had been more. Even if the way he was looking at her made her want to climb back into that sleeping bag. "I work much better when my stomach's not growling. I thought it might be the same for you."

"It is, but I'll cook. You made the coffee."

"That's because I can't work at all without caffeine."

"If I'd known that, I would've put on a pot as soon I got up."

"What time *did* you get up?" Judging by the sun's position, she swore it couldn't be any later than seven now. And, yeah, they'd agreed to start working at six.

"Maybe four?" he guessed, giving her a lazy smile.

"But it was almost two..." She let the sentence dangle, finishing the thought privately. She was quite sure he knew exactly what time they'd finally fallen asleep after he'd made love to her.

The question facing her now was where did this relationship—if you could even call it *that*—go from here?

* * * * *

Cardin and Trey are about to find out
that great sex is only the beginning....
Don't miss the fireworks!
Get ready for
A LONG, HARD RIDE
by Alison Kent.
Available March 2009,
wherever Blaze books are sold.

CELEBRATE
60 YEARS
OF PURE READING PLEASURE
WITH HARLEQUIN®!

We'll be spotlighting a different series
every month throughout 2009
to celebrate our 60th anniversary.

Look for Harlequin® Blaze™ in March!

0-60

*After all, a lot can happen in 60 years,
or 60 minutes...or 60 seconds!*

Find out what's going down in Blaze's
heart-stopping new miniseries *0-60!*
Getting from "Hello" to "How was it?"
can happen fast....

Look for the brand-new 0-60 miniseries in March 2009!

www.eHarlequin.com   HBRIDE09

You're invited to join our Tell Harlequin Reader Panel!

By joining our new reader panel you will:

- Receive Harlequin® books—they are FREE and yours to keep with no obligation to purchase anything!
- Participate in fun online surveys
- Exchange opinions and ideas with women just like you
- Have a say in our new book ideas and help us publish the best in women's fiction

In addition, you will have a chance to win great prizes and receive special gifts!
See Web site for details. Some conditions apply.
Space is limited.

To join, visit us at
www.TellHarlequin.com.

REQUEST YOUR FREE BOOKS!

2 FREE NOVELS PLUS 2
FREE GIFTS!

Love, Home & Happiness!

HARLEQUIN *Romance*®

This February the Harlequin® Romance series
will feature six Diamond Brides stories featuring
diamond proposals and gorgeous grooms.

Share your dream wedding proposal and you could WIN!

The most romantic entry will win a diamond
necklace and will inspire a proposal in one of
our upcoming Diamond Grooms books in 2010.

In 100 words or less, tell us the most romantic
way that you dream of being proposed to.

For more information, and to enter
the Diamond Brides Proposal contest, please visit
www.DiamondBridesProposal.com

Or mail your entry to us at:

IN THE U.S.: 3010 Walden Ave., P.O. Box 9069, Buffalo, NY 14269-9069
IN CANADA: 225 Duncan Mill Road, Don Mills, ON M3B 3K9

www.eHarlequin.com   HRCONTESTFEB09

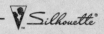

SPECIAL EDITION

TRAVIS'S APPEAL

by *USA TODAY* bestselling author

MARIE FERRARELLA

Shana O'Reilly couldn't deny it—family lawyer
Travis Marlowe had some kind of appeal. But
as Travis handled her father's tricky estate
planning, he discovered things weren't what
they seemed in the O'Reilly clan. Would
an explosive secret leave Travis and Shana's
budding relationship in tatters?

Available March 2009
wherever books are sold.

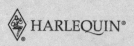 HARLEQUIN®

 *American ★ Romance*®

COMING NEXT MONTH
Available March 10, 2009

#1249 THE SHERIFF OF HORSESHOE, TEXAS by Linda Warren
Men Made in America
Quiet, friendly Horseshoe is the perfect place for Wyatt Carson to raise his young daughter. Until Peyton Ross zooms through his Texas hometown, disrupting his peaceful Sunday and turning his world upside down. The irrepressible blonde is tempting the widowed lawman to let loose and start living again. But there's more to this fun-loving party girl than meets the eye....

#1250 THE TRIPLETS' RODEO MAN by Tina Leonard
The Morgan Men
Cricket Jasper knows Jack Morgan's all wrong for her. But that doesn't stop the virtuous deacon from falling for the sexy rodeo rider. The firstborn Morgan son came home to make things right with his estranged father. Now *he's* about to become a father. Whoever dreamed it would take a loving woman with three babies on the way to catch this roving cowboy?

#1251 TWINS FOR THE TEACHER by Michele Dunaway
Times Two
Ever since Hank Friesen enrolled his son and daughter in Nolter Elementary, Jolie Tomlinson has been finding it hard to resist the ten-year-old twins...*and* their sexy dad. The fourth-grade teacher is happy to help out the workaholic widower—but getting involved with the father of her students is definitely against the rules. Besides, Jolie doesn't know if she's ready to be a mother—not until she tells Hank about her past....

#1252 OOH, BABY! by Ann Roth
Running a business and being a temporary mother to her sister's seven-month-old are *two* full-time jobs. The last thing Lily Gleason needs is to be audited! Then she meets her new accountant. Carter Boyle is handsome, single and trustworthy...and already smitten with Lily's infant niece. But the CPA has a precious secret—one that could make or break Lily's trust in him.

www.eHarlequin.com